MY HIGHLAND BRIDE

KINGDOMS OF MERIA BOOK 2

CECELIA MECCA

ALTIORA Press

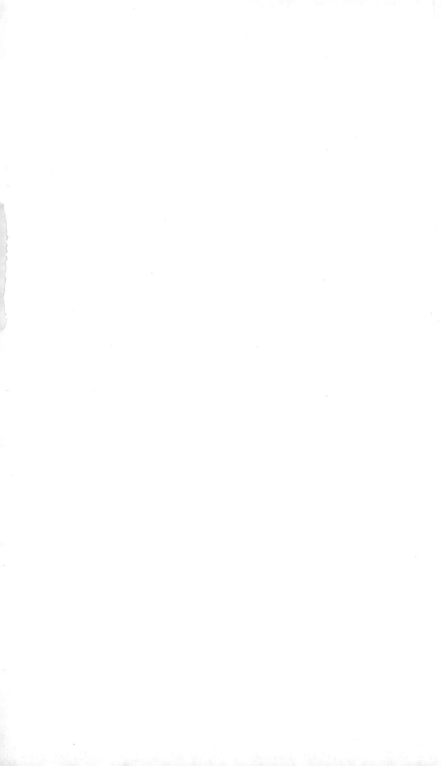

MY HIGHLAND BRIDE

A LEGENDS OF MERIA NOVEL

MY HIGHLAND BRIDE

Copyright © 2020 by Cecelia Mecca

Edited by Angela Polidoro

Cover Design by Najla Qamber Designs

All rights reserved.

To the most amazing group of beta readers. Thank you Elaine, Joanna, Margaret, Cindy and Lorrie.

ERIK

Breywood Castle, Kingdom of Edingham
    "Do you love her?"

The upper chamber of the gatehouse becomes completely quiet, and for good reason. It's an impertinent question—beyond impertinent—but I can almost admire my new squire for his bravery. Then again, the boy came to us from a small village a sennight ago, knowing nothing about knighthood, so perhaps he does not realize he is being brave.

"Did yer ma never teach you to shut yer mouth, boy?" scoffs Boyd, one of my guards.

Ignoring the boy's question, which I have found is the best approach, I say, "Boyd, the smith's son spotted a riding party on his way back from the village. He thought they might be from the king."

My squire jumps from his seat. "I met the king once!" he says, as excited as I've ever seen him. "I remember it, aye. The King of Meria."

Boyd and the others snicker.

"You met the king, did you?"

The guardsmen clearly do not believe young Bradyn. To

be fair, when he arrived at Breywood on the back of a cloth wagon, he hardly looked like a boy who'd once met a king.

"Do you remember his colors?" I ask him.

Bradyn nods eagerly. "Aye, Lord Stokerton. Red and gold."

The men still aren't impressed. Personally, I don't much care if Bradyn is being truthful or remembering incorrectly. If indeed the king's men are coming this way, I need to know immediately. A perfect job for an eager young squire.

"Climb up to the watchtower. As soon as you see red and gold banners approaching the gate, run to the training yard as fast as those two legs will carry you to tell me. Aye?"

"Aye, my lord."

Without waiting, he immediately does as he was bid, scrambling up the circular stone stairs.

"Why would the king's men come here?" Boyd asks as the others break away and go about their duties.

A good question. One I don't have an answer to. Our men, led by the first commander, Lord Scott, set out for the king's court to treat with him. Surely they have arrived by now, but would they have returned so quickly? And if so, why didn't the smith's son mention the two parties were traveling together?

"Could they be returnin' with Scott?"

I move to the slit on the westernmost wall and peer out. Nothing but grass and trees.

"He made no mention of the queen's banners."

Boyd grunts. "Is she aware we may have guests?"

"Nay, but I'm off to tell her now. She's at the yard. Make sure the boy sends word once he sees them."

This grunt, different from the last, tells me he's displeased. My choice of squire has raised his ire, which is too damn bad. Does my new squire ask too many questions? Aye. Does he know anything about being a squire? Nay.

But he jumped down from that wagon in the courtyard of Breywood Castle just after we had learned about the raid along the border that had seen his parents slaughtered. I hadn't thought to saddle myself with a squire again so soon after my last one received his spurs. Indeed, I'd vowed to remain squire-less for the foreseeable future, but I made the mistake of meeting the boy's eyes.

Besides, turning a homeless and parentless farmer's son into a knight is not the most difficult task I've ever undertaken.

I take my leave and begin walking toward the training yard. Though it would be faster to walk the allure, I need time to think on the implications of this royal visit from our longtime enemies.

After I met with King Galfrid's commander earlier this month, Cettina agreed to send a contingent to discuss terms with the king rather than mount an immediate counter-attack. Though the queen had the support of the Curia, many outside her inner council thought she was being soft.

They want war against Meria, always.

Especially after learning Galfrid sent two hundred of his best knights against us. That those men sunk to the bottom of the ocean in a shipwreck before arriving at our shores, the king's only son and heir one of them, matters little to the warmongers among us.

But the more I think on it, the less I believe these men have any connection to Lord Scott. Our banners have not been spotted. Which means these representatives of the king come of their own accord.

"Commander."

Nodding in greeting to the smith's apprentice, I hurry forward, anxious to speak with Cettina.

Do you love her?

I'll need to give Bradyn a talking-to. The rumors about

Cettina and me are persistent enough without any help. There is no need for my own squire to perpetuate them.

I hear the clang of swords before I see men at the quintain. Bradyn rotates between training in the yard, on the horse Cettina provided him, and with the men. He has a long way to go—others younger than he already display enough skill to see real battle—but I have every confidence he will rise to the challenge.

"Your shadow is missing," a young knight teases as I walk toward her.

"On guard duty," I respond, making my way toward the queen.

Her skill with the longsword grows more impressive each day. Cettina's insistence on learning to use it is just one of the many reasons we find ourselves the subject of flapping tongues.

Seeing me, she steps away from her opponent, hands him her sword, and nods to the edge of the yard. I meet her there, where it's slightly less noisy, and waste no time.

"The king's men have been spotted in the village. I assume they make their way here."

Cettina purses her lips together and looks me straight in the eye.

"Is Lord Scott with them?"

I shake my head.

"Our banners were not spotted." I glance down at her attire, similar to the other men in hose and a surcoat with no gown to be found. "I told Bradyn to fetch me as soon as they are spotted coming through the gates. Perhaps you should prepare for them."

She lifts her chin in defiance. One thing I've learned from serving Cettina is that she rarely does as she's willed. Not by me and not by her first commander, even though she trusts

Lord Scott implicitly. None of the Curia can compel the queen completely to their cause.

It is the reason I would give my life for her.

Unlike her father, she will do what she believes is right no matter the consequences. One day, I fear, such willfulness will get her killed. In the meantime, she is our best chance for returning Edingham to our ideals.

"I will meet them as such."

As the first queen of Edingham, or this Isle, Cettina has no precedents to follow. And apparently receiving her enemy's men in a tunic and hose will be an acceptable practice moving forward.

"Afterwards, we must talk," she adds.

"Your Grace?"

It annoys her when I use the title in private, and indeed, her eyes flash back at me.

"I know you returned from Murwood End talking of peace with Meria, but it will never come to pass unless we gain Lord Moray's support. Just yesterday my brother-in-law was seen speaking to MacKinnish."

My hands ball into fists. MacKinnish has little love for Cettina, and I even less for her bastard brother-in-law. I refrain from reminding Cettina that it was she who pardoned her excommunicated sister and brother-in-law and allowed them to return to the castle last year as one of her first acts as queen. I understand why she did it—her sister's treatment was unjust—but there's no denying Lord Whitley has been a pain in the arse ever since. He'll not rest until he's fully undermined Cettina.

"If we are to convince the Highlanders to stand down, we need Moray," she continues.

She's not wrong. Gaining Lord Moray's support for peace would placate the Highlanders and force those in Edingham who do not live in the mountains to follow, but unfortunately it will never happen. She knows this.

"He hates my family nearly as much as he does yours. Moray will never enter the fray, Cettina."

Again, that look. "There is no man the Highlanders will listen to more."

"We've dismissed this idea before."

"You and Scott have dismissed it, not I. Moray's support becomes ever more important as my brother-in-law stirs the Lowlanders. I will *not* be forced into war."

"Are you asking my advice as your commander, or are you ordering me to treat with him as my queen?"

I know the answer before she gives it.

"That, my dear Stokerton, is an official order."

Goddammit. It will be a waste of valuable time we do not have. Born and raised in the Highlands, I know they're much too stubborn to be convinced of anything against their will.

"Very well."

I bow as Cettina takes her leave. My family land borders Moray's, so at least I'll be able to pay a visit to my family.

"Oh," she calls back over her shoulder, "while you're there, perhaps you should enter so you might champion your queen. It would do well to remind everyone why you were chosen for this position."

I watch her walk from the yard toward the keep, trying to make sense of her words. Enter? Champion?

And then I remember.

2

REYNE

Ledenhill, Edingham

"Oh, Father, 'tis magnificent."

Though he doesn't answer, my father proudly scans the rows and rows of tents as if he organized the event himself. He didn't, of course. The Tournament of Loigh is commissioned by the Highland Council, with a new host chosen each year. There will be a sennight of eating and drinking and, for the participants, training, followed by a mock battle in which the two sides will compete to capture each other's warriors until just one man remains as champion. One uncaptured warrior who is not only honored at the tourney itself but for many years to come.

My father's look of ownership is because he has been champion more times than any other man. A fact he's reminded us of many times. So often, in fact, that Mother forbids him to mention it again.

As we continue to ride toward the colorful tents, which still do not rival the bright blue of the sky or the vivid green grass, I can feel Father studying me.

He's pleaded with me to attend for years, and for years I denied him. Until now. This day marks my first voyage from home since Fara died. My sister had always wished to attend the tournament, to see the Highland lords put forth their best men in a melee, but she was considered too young. So for years I stayed away, not wanting to experience what she could not. Now, at twenty and three, I am of an age that most would consider it odd that I have never been to a previous tournament.

"I wish Mother could have joined us for my first tourney."

"You may soon wish to be home with her, comfortable in your own bed," he calls as the men catch up behind us. More than a few of Father's men will be participating this year, and a few of them are good enough to be crowned champion.

I wish I'd have been brave enough to come before now. The fact is, since Fara died, I've been a coward. For nearly a year I refused to get close enough to the lake to even spy it from a distance. Even now, I will not go near its banks.

And since the voyage always requires river crossings, two to get to Ledenhill, I'd never even considered it until this year. Five years since Fara's death. Ten years of cowering at Blackwell. It was time.

"Do you see them, Reyne?"

I look down at the valley of tents and squint, trying to make out whichever figures he's noticed.

"Nay, there." He points past them, to the mountains.

"The mountains?"

"Aye." He sits up straighter in his saddle. "The very mountains where Aidan, son of Onry, fled all those years ago."

I try hard not to audibly sigh as my father launches into his most preferred speech of all, the tale of how Edingham was formed. My father is a man who enjoys his stories, but there is none he likes better than that of the prince who

8

avoided his father, the King of Meria, by hiding in the mountains. This tournament, held each year at the very spot where the Treaty of Loigh was signed after our bloody war for independence from the Kingdom of Meria, is considered a way of honoring and preserving the Highlanders' way of life.

Apparently sending a few dozen men after each other from opposite sides of a field to maim and capture their opponents is an ideal way to honor such a memory.

Men.

God save us from their stubbornness, my mother is fond of saying.

The sun is high by the time we descend into the valley. It is an unusually warm summer's day, full of promise. Though I attempt to assist the others in setting up our camp along the edge of the field full of tents, my efforts are mostly ignored. I do not, in fact, have any knowledge of how to erect a tent, as I've never slept in one. Nor have I been this far from Blackwell Castle before.

As I wonder how I should occupy myself, if not allowed to help, a hand goes around my waist. Startled, I scream until a familiar voice speaks my name, and I realize the perpetrator is none other than my brother.

"Warin!"

I spin around and toss my arms around my older brother. He squeezes me back, then holds me at arm's length.

"What are you doing here?" he asks, both surprised and mayhap a bit proud. Though only four years my senior, Warin often plays the role of a second father to me. A role to which I am accustomed, and for which I am at times grateful, at times annoyed. Right now, I cannot help but beam in delight under his scrutiny.

"Are you surprised?"

His hands still grip my shoulders.

"I could not be more surprised if the queen herself were standing before me."

Like our father, Warin has no great love for the queen. For Edingham, aye. But after Father had a falling-out with Queen Cettina's father, our family has remained as removed as possible from the politics of the capital.

"Were you frightened?"

"Aye," I admit. "The first crossing was not so bad. But the second." I close my eyes, thinking of how the water swirled around as we crossed. Visions of my beautiful sister bombarded me, so relentless my entire body was shaking by the time we reached the bank of the river. Father pulled me from my mount and held me in his arms as the others continued on their path.

For a man considered one of the greatest Highland warriors who ever lived, he was surprisingly free with his affections. It was the reason my mother fell in love with him, or so she says. Theirs was a love match, something few of their station could claim.

"Shh," Warin says, pulling me back to him. "Do not think on it. I'm proud of you, sister."

Love swells in my chest. He is so much like father in some ways, but he lacks the worst of Father's bluster. He is more quiet and thoughtful. But he's no less skillful as a warrior, and I suspect he'll be this tourney's champion. He deserves it. By the time my brother releases me, my hands have ceased their trembling.

"Why are you here?" I ask. "Father said you were still in Murwood End?"

My brother had a notion the year before to travel all of Meria before settling into his role as Father's successor, the next Lord Moray. We hadn't expected to see him here.

"I thought to surprise him. And I come with news from the North."

We look back toward the tents, Father now nowhere in sight.

"Likely three mugs into his ale." He points to a bright red tent. "Lord Beine."

"Ah, I hadn't seen the crest before."

A friend of father's, the Highland lord is notoriously short-tempered. I've never seen evidence of it myself, but one story places his temper as the catalyst for a battle that saw nearly half of his men killed.

The kind of friend one would not wish to make an enemy of, I suppose.

"What news from the North? Did you stay long in Murwood End? What is it like?"

Warin slings his arm around me as we walk toward our newly erected tents.

"The kind of news Father will not like," he says. "They say the king's Curia commander and Stokerton both paid Murwood End a visit at the same time."

I shield my eyes from the sun as we walk.

"A coincidence?"

Warin shrugs. "Perhaps. But after the Oryan sunk, calls for a counter-attack have only increased. It seems even the North is not immune to our fight."

"Our" fight, the never-ending border war with Meria.

"We've had more than one visitor over the past weeks, each asking for Father's support." I look up at my brother, who doesn't look surprised.

"He cannot avoid taking a stand forever."

I laugh. "Have you met our father?"

Warin steps over a puddle of mud, my skirts already worse for the wear, courtesy of yesterday's rains.

"I have. But even he may not be able to avoid the capital's troubles this time."

We shall find out soon enough. The very man in question

emerges from Lord Beine's tent. Seeing Warin, he raises his hand to wave just as his companion looks to the west. Suddenly, it seems everyone is doing so. I crane my neck but can see nothing for a time.

Then I realize what everyone stares at as the queen's bright blue and silver banners come into view.

3

ERIK

"Why do you not simply ask for an audience?" Gille asks, stretching out his legs as we sit in front of the tents.

After a day of wandering through the makeshift market and watching knights showcase their skill, as only one hundred men will be chosen for the melee, I am as impatient as Gille to speak to Lord Moray. I also know the man much better than my companion does.

Lord Gille Elliot, a Highlander whose family exerts considerable influence and whom I've come to rely on since being appointed second commander. Some might think him soft on account of his fondness for the finer things in life, but it was a mistake to assume so. A skilled tracker and fighter, he is one of Cettina's most valuable men.

As for Moray, I need to listen and learn first. The man must be approached with a fair measure of caution, or this journey will prove fruitless, and I am determined to find success here.

It is the least I can do after causing many of Cettina's current troubles.

"My lord?" We look toward the flap of the smallest of our three tents. Bradyn emerges with my mail in hand. "I've forgotten to bring sand for polishing."

Gille gives me a look, but I ignore it. If the boy is to learn, he won't do so back at Breywood without me.

"There's a barrel there"—I point toward the edge of camp —"for just that purpose."

Gille stretches out his legs, the canvas chair he sits on a luxury he insisted on bringing since we brought a wagon for the tents. For a man who wields a poleaxe like no other, he enjoys his comforts. Most of the men around us sit on the ground or, if they're lucky, a flat rock.

He's privileged, aye, but not soft. Gille Elliott is most unique.

"Aye, lord," Bradyn says, gamely shuffling off to the barrel.

The boy leaves us, and I cut off my companion before he can utter a word.

"His parents were killed. He has no one."

Gille scratches the back of his neck as he does whenever he has no good response.

"He will learn," I continue.

We both watch as the boy sidles up to other pages and squires crowding around the barrel of sand.

"Get in there," I mutter, as if he can hear me. "You bear the queen's crest."

"He won't do it," Gille says. "The boy is much too shy."

A temperament that will not serve him, or me, if he is to become a knight and serve the queen.

"Get in there," I urge him again.

Gille laughs at my silent coaching, but Bradyn squares his shoulders and edges his way toward the rim of the barrel. I beam at Gille as if the boy were my own.

"He's a long way from knighthood," he comments, "and a Highlander he'll never be."

I shrug. "Highlander. Lowlander. Voyager. Southerner. What does it matter?"

As two groups of men greet each other, their mood jubilant, so different from the tense atmosphere in the capital, Gille looks at me as if I'd just admitted to secretly being a Shadow Warrior.

"Have you never met a Merian you respected? A Voyager whom you trust? A Lowlander you might marry?"

I know the truth of that last one. Gille is unable to deny it.

"Of course. But that is a far cry from claiming it does not matter. You may wish it were not so, but you've been at the capital long enough to know otherwise."

Silence descends between us for a moment. He's right, and we both know it.

"So will you speak with him today?" he asks again.

I look toward the other edge of the camp, where Moray's flag billows in the wind. It's the only fully black one on the field, which makes it easy to distinguish.

He attends with his daughter and son, I've learned, though the son arrived separately. They say he has been traveling the Isle, though for what purpose none could say for certain. I've also learned Moray has not changed much in the time I've been away from home.

As always, he cares for one thing above all else.

His family.

Not the queen. Or the church. Or even his fellow Highlanders, whom he holds so dear. Nay, his highest loyalty is to the wife he married for love, the son he indulges, and the daughter he dotes on, even more so after losing poor Fara.

That was a dark day, for certain.

I was serving the queen as her personal guard when word of the poor girl's fate reached me in a letter from my mother. The fissure between our families meant I hadn't seen Moray or his girls for many years, but I felt their loss keenly. Fara's funeral marked the first time my father had spoken to Moray since the obstinate Highland lord had refused to support us in a battle that saw too many of our own men killed.

My father vowed never to forgive his neighbor for failing to send men to the Battle of Hendrelds Hill, and likely he never would. What started as a feud between two Highland families escalated when the king became involved, sending his own men to aid Lord Lemet's claim of land against Lord Carlsham. My father refused to battle against the king, even though he'd been an ally of both families and previously refused to enter the fight. As Moray had done.

Some said if Moray had sent men, Carlsham would have been quickly overwhelmed and surrendered. Instead, the battle became Edingham's bloodiest internal fight in our history, the fissures on both sides felt to this day.

Yet I was tasked with gaining support from that very man. If I thought being sent to Murwood End to gather support from the Voyagers in an attack on Meria was difficult, this would be even more so.

And it likely would have the same outcome.

"I will offer to fight for him," I say, proud of the solution I'd decided on this morn.

Each year a random draw saw two leaders chosen. All previous champions of the tourney had been guaranteed to fight on the side of their choice. All others would display their prowess in a series of activities, which would result in them being chosen for one side or the other . . . or eliminated from the competition altogether.

Some men had made their fortunes at such events, captured knights on both sides being ransomed for horses and riches and additional fees for recovered weapons.

"Aye."

And like him, I am one of only a handful of men who has been crowned champion of this tourney more than once.

There is a reason for it, and Moray would do well to have me on his side. He may not agree with my father or the queen, but he very much likes to win.

I suspect negotiations will go easier if we fight, at least for one day, for the same cause.

"I believe the queen was jesting when she told you to return as champion. Do you think she meant for us to stay here until the end of the tourney?"

It would be a sennight until the melee. A sennight away from the capital, not knowing what was happening back home.

"It does not matter. My charge was to get Moray's support, and I will do that any way I'm able."

"Including fighting in the melee?"

"Aye."

I would do that, and more, to win back Cettina's confidence. When the queen named me as second commander, my father had never been so proud. And then "the Hilla affair," its fallout, and the princess's disgrace. All because of me and my poor instincts.

Aye, I would do anything to find success here.

I stand.

"To Moray," I say. "'Tis time to get this done."

4

REYNE

*R*ubbing my temples, I return to my father's tent, now empty as the men have all gone off to the jousting field. Thankfully, I thought to bring a pouch of peppermint. I only hope it will work better this time than it did the last.

I find the satchel easily among my things. Heading back outside, I look toward the circle of rocks with the cold wood gathered inside, wishing there were still a fire so that I might boil some water. I could chew the peppermint, but I've found drinking it works better.

Though I've never started a fire on my own before, I've watched the men do it on this journey and am sure I can manage it easily. After retrieving a knife from the tent, I pick up a rock and bend down in front of the pile of wood, striking the knife repeatedly against the metal as I've seen Father's men do.

I see sparks but nothing more.

"You've missed a few steps there, my lady."

I shoot up and spin around toward the voice.

Forgetting my poor attempts at making a fire, I stare at

the stranger before me. He is, quite easily, the most handsome man I've ever met.

He is even taller than my father and brother. And wider in the shoulders. A Highlander, aye. But his hair is shorter, more like a Southerner. Or a man of court, likely one who arrived under the queen's banner.

I don't know him, but there is something vaguely familiar about the man.

"I . . ." Words fail me before they return in a rush. "I've never started a fire before."

The queen's man takes a step toward me. I should be afraid to find myself alone with him. I promised Father not to go anywhere without an escort, but when I could not find any of his men unoccupied, I decided to return to the tent on my own.

"I can see that."

His smile demands a response. Although embarrassed to have been caught as such by a noble guardsman, I manage to collect myself. I toss the rock back onto the pile and slip the knife into the fold in my gown. His eyes fall to the pouch of herbs still clutched in my hand.

"Peppermint?"

My eyes widen. How could he know such a thing?

"Aye."

It is a wonder I can speak at all. I've asked my mother, many times, to tell me the story of how she met Father. Always she tells me this: the moment he stepped into the hall, she was struck silent by the sight of him. Even now, she finds him the most handsome man in existence. The guardsman reaches for my hand. "May I see it?"

He wants to see my peppermint?

"Did you pick it in early bloom but when no more new leaves were being formed?"

I take a stem out and attempt to hand it to him but am

19

mortified to realize my fingers are trembling. Does he notice as I drop it into his hand? Surely he does.

"What do you use it for?" he asks, examining it.

Since it feels odd to confess a headache to a stranger, I grapple for an appropriate answer. But it seems I've taken too long.

"You've nothing to fear from me, Lady Reyne."

"How do you know my name?" I ask, startled.

He gives me the look of one who knows me, but I am assured we have not met. I would remember such a man clearly.

Standing back and bowing so very properly, still grinning, he introduces himself.

"Erik Stokerton, at your service, my lady."

I gasp. Could this be the very same Erik Stokerton who once marched into our hall claiming he was no longer the son of Bern but would prefer to be a Moray instead? My excitement of having a new brother was quickly squashed when my father promptly set the tall, skinny neighbor's son on his horse and rode him immediately home, explaining that he could not choose a new father simply because he disliked the number of hours he was made to sit with his tutor.

That was before the Battle of Hendrelds Hill, of course, after which I never saw Erik again.

"You are not a queen's guardsman," I accuse, even though Erik had not specifically claimed to be. I'd drawn that conclusion all on my own.

"Nay," he says cheekily, "I am not."

He is the queen's second commander, the youngest in the Curia's history. Former champion of this tourney. Edingham's most famous warrior, he fought a contingent of Merians so fiercely he was hailed by Cettina's father, King Malcom, on the battlefield, brought immediately to court, and named as personal guard to the princess.

This cannot be the same boy I knew. And yet his smile is the same. Erik's smile always reached his eyes, even as a boy.

"'Tis really you."

He hands back my peppermint.

"Shall I be offended you did not recognize me when I knew who you were right away?"

I gesture toward our tents. "You had an advantage, Erik." I immediately correct myself, "Lord Stokerton."

"You will not use my given name because our fathers are two stubborn old goats?"

A truth if I've ever heard one.

"I will not use your given name because you are a Curia commander and 'twould not be proper to do so."

"Come here, Reyne."

We are much too close now, considering he is no longer a boy but an immensely handsome man, but I do as he asks anyway.

As bold now as he was then, he snatches the pouch from me and tosses it to the ground.

"What are you about?"

And then he takes my hands. Gasping, I attempt to pull away. But he holds them steady, turning both over so my palms face upward. As if that were not improper enough, he starts massaging my hands, focusing on the area between the thumb and forefinger.

"Close your eyes," he bids.

I do it, unable to believe this gorgeous stranger is not a stranger at all but Erik Stokerton, the queen's commander. And, if the rumors are true, her lover as well.

"I assume the peppermint is for a headache?" Erik asks, still massaging my hands in that very strange spot.

"Aye." I've had them since childhood but am surprised he

remembered, and even more surprised he so quickly connected the peppermint to my ailment.

"If we were successful in starting a fire to boil water, it would not have helped much. You must choose stems with more leaves and, as I mentioned, be sure to pick them in early bloom. The ones you have would not prove very potent."

As he continues his ministrations, I actually begin to feel a bit better.

"This is a more effective treatment if the pain is not substantial."

His fingers are rough, not surprising for a warrior's hand, but they're also gentle. Suddenly remembering where we are, and the possibility one of the men could come along at any time, I open my eyes.

Surely I misinterpret the look he is giving me. This is a man in love with a queen, a woman whose beauty none deny even if they do not care for her.

"Does your head feel any better?"

I swallow and nod, not trusting my voice to answer.

Dropping my hands, he nods. "Good. I'm glad to hear it. And would be even more glad to hear my name from your lips. We were, after all, nearly siblings once."

Again, his smile is infectious.

"Very well, Erik. Though not so nearly, I fear. My father was not very pleased with your pronouncement."

He laughs. "You should have seen my own father if you think yours was angry."

Spying a hulking figure approaching us from a distance, I take a step back, away from Erik.

"Since we speak of angry fathers, you should know one is headed this way."

But Erik does not flinch. He does not even look off toward the game fields.

"Good, as he is the reason I'm here."

Of course, I know he had not come just to greet me, but his words sting nonetheless. Still, my father's face comes into view. He is staring at Erik and, as usual when the name Stokerton is raised, he does not look very pleased.

To think I'd just gotten rid of my headache. It seems another might not be far behind it.

5

ERIK

*A*s I wait for Moray, his daughter distances herself from me. A pity, as I rather enjoyed standing so close to her.

Though I had the advantage of knowing I was surrounded by Moray tents, I would have recognized her anywhere. Once, as a boy, I asked my father why Lord Moray's son did not have that vivid red hair, bright enough to be spied from across a crowded hall, like he and his daughter. I don't recall his answer, but it would be impossible to forget that color. Or the flashing eyes that accompanied it. They'd taunted me into trouble every time my family visited Blackwell Castle. She'd always reminded me of a flame, dashing and dancing, dangerous and powerful.

Seeing her alone outside of the tent, I'd forgotten my mission for a brief moment—distracted by her beauty, and by the mystery of how she could look both the same and also entirely different. I felt compelled to touch her, both because of the headache and because I wanted to, but it is probably not something I should do again if these negotiations are to go well.

And that is what I am here for. Negotiations. Not, however pleasant as it might be, to become reacquainted with a childhood friend.

"Stokerton."

His voice is deep and commanding, just how I remember it.

"Lord Moray." I bow though I am not required to do so. "A pleasure to see you again."

There is a reason Moray is so powerful among the Highland lords, and it is not as simple as the land he has amassed, which is considerable, or his reputation as a respected warrior, which is indisputable. Nay, people respect him for his refusal to send his warriors into a conflict he does not believe in.

Though my father is not one of them.

According to him, Moray's obstinacy came at too high a cost. Men died because he refused to join the fight, leaving the burden to my father and other lords.

Do you follow your leader even if you know they are wrong?

For Moray, the answer is nay. For my father, it has always been aye.

As for me? I am still undecided on that count. I don't expect I'll ever have to decide, for Cettina is a better queen than her father was a king. Her sister had been raised to take on that role, but I was convinced the right Borea inherited the crown. Before being named commander, I was Cettina's personal guard, so I have known her for years. Which means I know what many are coming to learn.

She is worthy of the title Queen of Edingham.

But Moray knows none of this. He clearly sees me and the man who sired me as one and the same. My job here will be to convince him otherwise. To persuade him to treat with me despite his animosity toward my family.

"A pleasure? I would say the same if I knew your purpose here at my tents, alone with my daughter."

"Father!"

I do not blame the man for his suspicions.

"I came here looking for you and happened upon Lady Reyne."

He grunts and addresses his daughter. "You missed your brother. He just won the stone throw."

I am not surprised. Warin has long been one of the strongest men I know.

"I am sorry to have missed it," she says, looking down.

The conciliatory response surprises me. I do not remember Reyne as the sort to defer to anyone, even her father. The woman Reyne is much more subdued than I remember.

"I would speak to you," I finally manage as the Highland lord turns his attention back to me. Only one of his men accompanied him from the field, and any fool could see how he looks at Reyne.

Moray gestures toward the biggest of the cluster of tents. While most of the occupants are off at either that day's games or the makeshift market that springs up for the tournament, a few stragglers, including ourselves, remain.

Following Moray into the tent, I glance back and give his man a look of warning. I've no right to do so, of course, but I doubt Reyne or her father would appreciate his leering if they were to notice. For his part, the man seems surprised by my interference.

"I'd have thought you too busy at court to come here," Moray says, taking a seat and gesturing for me to do the same. This tent, unlike my own, is not for sleeping but for entertaining. The table is equipped with a pitcher and mugs and candleholders for the evening, surrounded by four chairs, nicer than the low slingback ones Gille insisted on bringing. It must have required at least two separate wagons to bring the furnishings for this one tent.

Moray never did do anything in half measures.

I accept his offer of wine and then sit.

"I've been kept busy," I admit, "with Galfrid's attempted attack and the return of the queen's sister and brother-in-law." The latter I admit only because of my family's history with this man. Moray and my father may no longer be allies, but I can trust him. That much I know well.

"'Tis true, then? The rumors of Whitley's meddling?"

"Aye, 'tis true enough."

Moray grunts. "Once a bastard . . ."

He has no love for the man, nor for any of the border lords, from what I can remember.

"And Galfrid? Does the queen intend to strike back at him?"

So much for idle chatter.

"The course forward is still undecided. There are many factors at play."

King Galfrid seems genuinely interested in peace. Having lost his son and heir, he has larger problems than the never-ending conflict between our nations. And with his men in Breywood opening discussions with Cettina, and ours in Meria's capital, I think it almost possible.

But only if the Highlanders fall into line.

"That is why I am here. I must speak to you about the future," I say.

Before he answers, I realize I've not spoken to him since Fara's death.

"I am sorry for your loss, Moray. I would have come to the funeral had I not been detained at the capital."

A shadow crosses his expression, though briefly, and a quick nod is the only indication he's heard me.

"I bear no grudge against you, lad."

Though it's been some time since I've been called as such, I hold my tongue.

"Neither do I wish your father ill," he continues. "But you traveled a long way for naught. I will not encourage the Highland lords to stand down."

I don't flinch at his correct assessment of the situation.

"Do some believe King Galfrid's actions cannot stand?" he asks. "Aye. Do I wish to involve myself in the capital's politics? Nay. Never again. I've no interest in the king's troubles. No one thinks much of his nephew, but it matters naught to me whom he chooses as heir."

Stubborn old goat. Elric Hinton would be a nightmare for Meria, and for us too, yet the church is committed to seeing him installed as the heir. They've gone so far as to say it is God's will.

"The capital's politics are yours," I start out, but Moray shakes his head.

"Spoken like your father."

That is where he is wrong.

"I don't blame you for not sending men to fight in a battle of King Malcom's making. But surely you can see what King Galfrid's troubles would bring to our shores? Many of our people claim 'tis time to strike Meria. But if the church is successful in installing a man such as Hinton to the throne, 'twill cause problems for all of us. And do you not fear Father Silvester's increased influence?"

As the Prima and leader of the church, Father Silvester has more than once used his Shadow Warriors to exert influence he should not have. Left unchecked, the man would surely wreak havoc well beyond Meria's borders.

"Malcom embraced the man," Moray says of Silvester.

"The queen does not," I insist. "She has no love for a man who cares more for his own power and influence than for the people who so dutifully follow him."

"What does the queen want?" Moray asks.

A fair question.

"Peace," I say, unequivocally.

Moray snorts. "We've never had peace on the Isle and never will."

I can't help but smile. "For a man so at odds with my father, you sound remarkably like him."

Moray doesn't budge.

"I will not become involved. The Council can make decisions for itself."

He drinks, so I do as well. Having expected this response, I try another angle.

"If Whitley keeps stirring up trouble along the border, she will be pressed into a war that will not serve Edingham . . . unless she has enough support to prevent it."

"She should not have allowed him back."

Him being Cettina's brother-in-law. And while I agree, I cannot say as much. Lord Whitley has been making trouble for years, his every action guided by his thirst for power. The two were sent away after Cettina's sister, Lady Hilla, had an affair. Or possibly had the affair. She never admitted to it, and the king beheaded the man who was supposedly involved. I personally think King Malcom had grown quite mad. Near the end of his life, he railed more and more often against his enemies, real and imagined, losing even his most loyal supporters, like my father.

He damaged the kingdom, and now it is up to Cettina, with the Curia's help, to repair it.

"Lady Hilla is the queen's sister." I take another sip, biding my time. I need him comfortable for my proposal to be considered. "She could not bring her back without reinstating her husband too. Lord Whitley is the price she pays for supporting her sister."

"A pity." Moray makes another sound low in his throat

before drinking deeply from his goblet. "But as I said, I cannot help you."

Ah, but he could. If Moray ordered the others to cease their instigations of war, they would listen. At least for a time. And if Cettina is able to avoid another war, perhaps Edingham could unite long enough to repel any designs Father Silvester has on increasing his power here as he is doing in Meria. Many of the Eldermen who serve him agree privately that the church's current corruption stems from one person alone: the man in charge. When the Prima is gone—and the man seems older than my father and Moray together—there may be a real chance for lasting peace.

"I met with the king's commander in Murwood End," I tell him, laying most of my cards on the table for Moray to see.

"And did the Voyagers pledge to join you if a battle becomes inevitable?"

In fact, they did not. The fierce ship captains of Murwood End are steadfast in their neutrality. More's the pity. Except I find that I wish for peace more than I do for victory.

"We hope it does not come to that."

"It will." Moray finishes his wine and stands to refill his goblet. "It always does."

Ignoring him, I forge ahead. "Commander d'Abella believes peace is achievable."

Moray snorts. "Of course he does. Now that they lost a ship full of their best fighters, along with the heir to the throne. I'm sure he is desperate for it."

I find myself defending Galfrid's commander.

"Would we not do the same if over half a village was slaughtered in the dead of night? The Borderlands must be contained."

"And the queen proposes to do that by unleashing Lord Whitley?"

He raises a good point. The once-powerful border lord has regained some of his former influence now that his lands have been restored. I understand Cettina's reasoning—punishing Whitley also punishes her sister—but I wish she'd listened to the Curia's advice.

A right mess, without a doubt.

"Whitley will be controlled."

Moray looks as skeptical as I feel.

"But we need the Highlanders' support." Time to make my offer. "I will fight for you in the tournament. Cettina is prepared to offer you a large sum of gold as well."

Sitting back, he actually seems to consider my offer. The gold would not be motivation enough for Moray. Backing Cettina will not garner him any favors with the other Highlanders . . . but he also desires to win here. Perhaps he wants it enough to tip the scales.

Suddenly, without warning, Moray smiles. The hairs on my neck rise up. I cannot remember the man smiling so broadly before, and my stomach lurches at the implications.

Slamming his goblet on the table, Moray leans forward and plants a hand on each knee.

"I care little for gold."

I do not like his expression.

"But you do wish for your side to be victorious here?"

"I do. And it will." A pause. "But I wish for something else more."

I imagine Moray meeting with the Council at this very tournament. Returning to the capital to tell Cettina she has their support against those whose calls for war grow increasingly shrill.

I would give him anything.

"Name it."

"I would see Reyne wed."

I blink, unsure I've heard correctly.

"I would see our lands united, despite your father's stubbornness."

Moray's land borders ours, and such a union would be advantageous to both families.

I think of Reyne. Of her as my wife. I've not considered the possibility before, but the idea is not without merit.

I also think of how Cettina might react.

"Wed my daughter. Unite our lands. I would welcome a man such as you into our family."

Though honored and intrigued by the possibility, I do wonder one thing.

"How will Reyne feel about such an arrangement?"

That's when Moray's smile returns.

"She will not like it. Reyne believes in love," he scoffed like the idea was absurd. "And has been resistant to the idea of marriage. I fear that my wife and I are to blame."

All know the Morays' marriage was a love match, which is why his disdain for his daughter's wishes is curious.

"And I've been indulgent since . . ."

He stops, but I know what he meant to say. Since Fara's death.

"It is time."

Was I really going to agree to such a thing? I did not come here to bargain for a wife, but one such as Reyne might be welcome. My father would be angry at first, but even he could be made to see the wisdom of uniting our lands. And this one act would win the Highland lords' support for Cettina. And not just on this one issue, but for all time.

There is only one answer in the end.

"I will do it."

"Ah. . ." Moray waves his finger in the air. "I did not explain my stipulation yet. One you'll find difficult to meet."

"Which is?"

Moray appears even more amused than ever.

"You will have to get Reyne to agree first."

6

REYNE

"*I*s Father acting strangely today?"

Warin appears less comfortable here in the market than he did earlier, attempting to cut down fellow Highlanders. I will admit, though I enjoyed my first full day at the tourney, I was not prepared for the violence of the games.

I've seen our men train many times. But this was different. While they fought with blunted weapons, they wielded them with a vigor that had made me nervous for my brother.

"I don't believe so," Warin answers.

As we stroll through the wooden market stalls erected for this tournament, passing everything from fruits to fabrics, Warin doesn't seem to notice the appreciative glances the ladies are giving him—their attention more on him than the wares. A handsome man, he has never before mentioned marriage, although as the eldest sibling and heir to Blackwell, he will be duty bound to marry someday.

"Have you thought of marriage lately?" I ask.

It isn't something we've discussed in a long while, given

Warin has spent so much time away on his quest to "discover the Isle."

"Rarely," he says, giving me a look brimming with curiosity. "What makes you consider such a thing? Has Father mentioned it?"

I stop at a stand with two women behind it. Their table includes many things, from wax to jewelry, which is obviously handmade.

Since I cannot admit that the subject occurred to me after my encounter with Erik Stokerton earlier that day, I shift my focus to the vendors and inquire about their hair pins.

"I would like this one," I say, picking up a lovely bronze pin topped with an intricate carving. "Is this what it appears?"

The younger of the two leans forward to see which one I've chosen.

"Aye, that is the Kona," she responds. A closer examination reveals she is correct. Which is when I notice the small gem in the woman's nose. Saying nothing more than asking for the cost, I hand her a coin and take the pin with me.

"They were Garra," I whisper to Warin, trying not to look back.

He does not seem to be as impressed as I am.

"Did you hear me?"

I've missed my brother's smile.

"Aye, Reyne, I heard you."

"I forgot I'm speaking with Warin the traveler, and not Warin the boy who once got himself into trouble for sneaking into the hall to see King Malcom's commander. You were as sheltered as I am."

"I met a Garra in Murwood End," he says. "She was like any other woman."

Nay, not exactly like any other woman. The Garra are

35

special healers, loathed by the church and loved by most of the common people, and some say they have powers well beyond those of a physician or healer.

"Speaking of a king's commander . . ." He looks down at me, but there is nowhere to hide the flush on my cheeks.

He whistles. "So it is true. Rory said you were keen on him, but I didn't believe it. I remember Erik as a skinny boy who was always tripping over his own feet."

The sound I make is less than ladylike.

"He is not such any longer, I take it?"

Erik Stokerton is neither skinny nor awkward. Of course, my brother already knows as such. While they may not have fought together, all in the Highlands know Lord Stokerton's son was awarded a position at court for his bravery on the battlefield. Besides which, the two have fought against each other in this very tournament. My brother's side lost. Nay, he is surely not the same boy we knew when our fathers were allied.

"No answer?"

I'd give one, but the subject of our discussion stands a short distance before us. Erik and his companion are facing one of the booths, speaking to the merchant, although I can't see what he or she is selling. There are more women here than in the fields.

This could be any marketplace except that it has been erected in the courtyard of the host castle. As of yet, Blackwell has not had the honor of hosting the tournament. Father does not wish for it, truthfully, for the tournament is a drain on the host's coffers.

"Why have we stopped?" asks my brother.

"Because."

It's not my most eloquent answer ever.

"Moray?"

We both turn as someone calls my brother's name from behind.

"Lord Beine. I've been told you lurked here at the tourney somewhere."

The two shake hands and hardly notice as I slip away. Lord Beine's son and my brother are old friends, just like our fathers, and I have little desire to stay for their idle chatter. Fara always accused me of being unfriendly, although that is not precisely true. I just do not care to speak to everyone and anyone. I would prefer to keep company with our family. Or our tutor. Or even with myself, if the alternative is exchanging empty pleasantries.

But not Fara. She loved being around people. Talking to them. Laughing with them. Dancing. Singing. She was the brightest star in the sky, always glittering even when all others were dimmed for the night.

"This is a tournament, a place to be joyful, Reyne."

I didn't even notice him approach. But as he does, my heartbeat quickens.

"Lord Stokerton."

He rolls his eyes, smiling. "Erik, please."

It seems odd to call him that, even though I've known him for years. He is a Curia commander now, the third most important person in Edingham after the queen and her first commander. His surcoat with the official blue tree of Edingham is a reminder, as if I needed one, that this is not the boy I knew. He is all man.

"You did not enter in any of the day's events?"

One thing that has not changed is Erik's smile.

I point to his pristine surcoat. "This may be my first tourney, but I've seen many men who've competed, and none look quite so clean."

Erik crosses his arms."Perhaps I've changed clothing?"

He's teasing me, reminding me we are not strangers.

"I did not see you on the lists."

"Were you looking?"

My surprise at the question stops me from answering. Which, of course, is all the answer he needs.

"I was not," I insist.

Though Erik is not the first man who has flirted with me, he is certainly the first one who has made me want to crawl under one of the merchant's tables and hide. I've no notion how to act with a man who makes my stomach twist up each time he looks at me thus.

"Hmm." He looks down at my hand. "Have you made a purchase?"

Thankful for the change in subject, I show him the pin.

"The woman who sold it to me was a Garra."

He moves closer, to look at the hairpin of course, but when he does so, awareness washes over me. My body comes alive in a way I'd not believed possible.

"There is a woman, a Garra, who lives in the capital," he says, inspecting the pin. "I've spoken to her more than once."

I show him the carving of the mini Kona on top, curious now about Erik's visits to the Garra. They can treat a variety of ailments, but their focus is on love and romance, which is the reason for the church's contempt. It is said they can cure a broken heart or make a man or woman fall in or out of love. Did he visit the Garra because of the queen? All know of his attachment to her. Rumors of Cettina and her commander have reached my ears more than once, even when the king was still alive, when Erik was the then-princess's personal guard.

"Does this truly give the Garra her power?" I ask, having heard the real Kona, a yarn doll passed from mother to daughter, does that very thing.

"I do not believe so," he says, looking at the pin. "But that is a remarkably intricate carving." He looks up then, his eyes a deep blue, like the sea. "I am sorry about your sister," he says suddenly. "I'd have come to her funeral had I been able to leave the capital."

Her funeral was the only occasion Erik's father and mine have come together since their disagreement. All of the Highland lords and ladies came, a show of support like none I'd ever seen.

"Thank you," I say.

I glance back at Warin, and although he is still in conversation with Lord Beine's son, he has clearly noticed I am talking with Erik.

"You said you've not been to a tournament before," he says to me, jolting my attention back to him. "Not even this one?"

"Nay."

I don't wish to admit the reason, so instead I ask a question of my own. Something I've wondered about since this morning.

"Why are you here? These are uncertain times, from what I understand. Surely you are needed back at Breywood?"

Erik glances over my shoulder, and when he responds, pointedly avoiding my first question, his tone is less warm. "I am needed here as well. Good day, Warin."

I hadn't noticed my brother's approach.

"Erik."

Unlike me, Warin immediately takes Erik's cue to use his given name. It is so very like a man not to question himself. My father is the same way, even when some circumspect thinking would be to his benefit.

"My father told me that he spoke to you earlier."

"Aye, that he did."

I'm not sure I understand the look Erik gives Warin, as if questioning him, but it fades when Warin reaches out his hand. "It has been too long."

In response, Erik takes it and pulls him close. As the men embrace, I watch with fascination. What just happened there?

Erik slaps Warin on the back as they stand apart. "I've heard of your travels," he says. "It seems we missed each other in Murwood End."

"You were there recently?" Warin asks, surprised.

"Aye."

He does not elaborate, and my brother does not ask him to. Instead, he asks, "Will you be at the feast tonight?"

The Lord Ledenhill will host a feast this eve, according to Father. Our whole family will be there, and it seems that Erik may attend as well.

Do not overexcite yourself over the possibility. He is the queen's man, not yours.

But my mind and body do not seem to be speaking to each other. I await impatiently, heart thudding, for Erik's answer.

"Will *you* be at the feast, Reyne?" he asks me.

If I had thought Erik flirted with me earlier, the look he gives me now confirms it. Curiously, Warin does not seem affected. Every potential suitor who has attempted to so much as speak with me has been the subject of my brother's intense scrutiny. But here is the son of a man Father dislikes enough to avoid the western borders of our land, and Warin says nothing. Does nothing.

I will have to question him about his behavior. But first, to address Erik's question.

"Aye," I say, "I plan to attend."

As if confirming my suspicions, Erik brightens. "I look

forward to it. Forgive me for intruding on your walk," he says to us both. "Until this eve, then?"

Bowing slightly and attracting a fair measure of attention with his mere presence, Erik walks away. And I do not waste any time addressing my brother's odd behavior.

"Would you like to tell me what just happened, Warin?"

7

ERIK

*L*edenhill Castle, built partially into the side of the mountains, surrounded by rocky peaks on three sides, is in some ways more magnificent than Breywood. Our capital is along the sea, beautiful in its own way, but a Highlander born is a Highlander for life, and I have always preferred the mountains.

But as I enter Ledenhill's glittering hall, the sounds of music and revelry flowing over me, it's not the castle I'm thinking about but the woman who holds my fate—some would say *Edingham's* fate—in her hands.

Though she does not know it yet.

Moray is doubtful she will agree to the union, however he wishes otherwise, and has said as much. If she balks, he will honor her wishes . . . and I will leave without his support. He is adamant that she will not agree to an arranged marriage, so I must convince her she wishes to marry me. He was very clear on one point: I'm not to dishonor her in any way. I replied that I valued my life too much to try it.

"You are a bigger fool than Lord Bowes," Gille says as we enter the hall together.

Lady Hilla's decapitated lover has become synonymous with foolish, reckless decisions. But my role in the affair's discovery is not one I wish to be reminded of at this particular moment. Of course, Gille does not know all.

"You do not think I can convince her?"

Our hosts are already seated on the dais as their guests, easily more than one hundred men and women, mill about. Some begin to sit as others flit from table to table, greeting their friends and neighbors. Fiddlers give the hall a festive atmosphere completely at odds with the current tense mood in the capital.

Being here, I can understand Moray's ambivalence toward the queen's dilemma. It all feels very far away. But he's mistaken if he thinks even the wildest corners of the Highlands are safe. Meria's influence can be felt even here, and the Prima's power spreads throughout both kingdoms like disease through a tree.

Some eye us with suspicion. Others, with respect. If I've learned anything from my years in the capital, it is that some men will defer to a position more than they will a man or woman, and others will do just the opposite.

"Do you wish to marry her?" Gille's question jolts me out of my thoughts.

"I do not wish to marry anyone. But as my mother tells me in nearly every missive, I've no siblings to carry on the Stokerton name." I am lucky to be alive, my birth not an easy one for my mother. Afterward, she was never able to become pregnant again. "So if I must marry, 'tis as good a reason as any."

"To please the queen?"

Gille knows by now that I won't respond. He accepts a goblet from a serving maid, and we make our way through the crowd, Gille enjoying his drink while I search for Reyne.

I spot her father first and then . . . and then the bright red hair of the woman standing next to him with her back turned to us.

"There," I say, walking toward her. As we do so, she turns.

"In the name of the Prima," he mutters. "One man cannot be so lucky."

His reaction is much the same as mine was earlier in the market. I hadn't expected to see her, and the jolt I felt was unexpected. Reyne's beauty is wild. Untamed. Were she at court, those slight freckles across her brow would be covered with powder. Her full lips accentuated with unnecessary color. Though she is not as refined as the ladies who flock to Breywood Castle, she is lovelier for it.

"I'll do it," Gille says. "Surely Moray would be equally as pleased to ally with my family."

He's jesting, surely, and I don't point out that the Morays and Elliots are already in good standing, a fact he knows well.

When we reach the Morays, Gille plays the charming courtier almost immediately, not even waiting for an introduction.

"It is an honor to make your acquaintance, Lord Moray. Sir Gille Elliot." He juts out his hand. Moray gives me a slightly startled look, but he takes it, giving Gille his attention. "You've met my father, Lord Elliot. And you must be Lady Reyne."

It's only when he takes her hand and kisses it that I realize he was not jesting.

Both father and daughter are taken in by the lout, who pretends I'm not standing next to him. Not only have Gille's father and Moray met, Gille reminisces, but they hunted together in the spring. I watch the exchange with some amount of amusement, until Reyne sneaks a glance at me.

And suddenly, I'm no longer amused.

Her long lashes brush her cheeks as she gazes at me. For a

moment I think she wishes to say something, but Gille steals her attention away. He has shifted to regaling them with stories about his own hunting escapades. Reyne laughs and smiles, and I find my good nature is overcome with . . .

Anger?

Nay, I am not usually quick to anger. Jealousy? Perhaps, but only because Gille has made a practice of stealing attention.

"Was that the same hunting excursion," I interrupt, "when you were shot in the arse with an arrow?" Reyne nearly spits out her wine. "Pardon, my lady, if my words offend you."

"It was not," Gille says, as affronted as if the woman he's attempting to charm is not the very same one I've agreed to marry. "And well you know it, *Commander*. Were you not present the day your squire shot me?"

Indeed I was.

I have a history of fostering squires none deem adequate to train. Which reminds me of Bradyn, whom we left back in the tents. Servants, squires, and pages, though not invited to the hall, typically hold their own feast of sorts. I tried to prepare Bradyn for the kind of revelry awaiting him this eve. How does he fare?

"We've obviously much to discuss. Would you sit with us this eve?" I direct the question both to Moray and Reyne, looking between the two. If I've learned one thing from Cettina, it is that a woman does not take kindly to being talked over.

My mother may have her own mind in many things, but it is the queen who truly showed me the traditional gender roles in our society needn't be that way. Women and men are given equal status in Murwood End, and she aims to make it so here as well. Much of the current dissent has less to do with Cettina's policies than her gender.

Reyne looks to her father, who nods.

45

"Warin will be joining us as well," she says, looking toward the table set closest to the dais. It is the only one with Edingham's banner, the Tree of Loigh, draped down the side.

"I look forward to meeting him," Gille interjects.

Likely not as much as I look forward to speaking with my friend alone. For now, it seems, I'll content myself with the company of a potential ally, a potential wife and brother-in-law, and, very likely, an ex-friend and comrade.

Gille laughs at the look I give him, and I cannot help but smile along with him. Looking at Reyne now, can I truly blame him for trying? She is lovely and charming, and I find myself warming to the idea of marrying this woman I knew in childhood.

Moray says she will not marry me if she knows about our talk . . . but I have given it thought, and I cannot bring her to the altar without telling her. Charm her, aye. Fool her, nay. My hope is that by the time this tournament has ended she will have gotten to know me well enough not to care how the match came to be.

The nagging voice in the back of my head urging me to tell her now? I shove it aside despite the advice my father has given me many times.

That feeling inside here, he'd say, pointing to my chest, *that is the one you must trust.*

Sometimes, I've learned since leaving home, that feeling can lead you astray.

8

REYNE

"I cannot look."

Sitting with Warin on the wooden stands and watching as Erik takes his place, axe in hand, I feel the urge to cover my eyes. Aside from the melee, the Triumph is one of the most prestigious events at this tourney, but it is also one of the most dangerous. Our uncle was badly injured years ago on this very field the last time this tourney was held at Ledenhill. Since then, my father has skipped it each year. Warin doesn't participate either.

I recognize the dangers of the melee are just as great, but logic does not seem to play a role when it comes to this tourney. Or, in fact, in many things Highlander men hold dear.

And yet, two days after arriving at Ledenhill, I am enjoying myself more than I would have thought possible. Aside from some lewd stares and even a few comments that made my ears turn pink, these past few days have been some of the best of my life.

The sense of camaraderie among the Highland families is unmistakable. Blackwell has hosted gatherings and feasts in the past, but none compare to the scope of this tourney. According to Warin, the melee on the last day is the greatest event of all, but if we left now I would be happy.

And then there is Erik.

Last eve, he and Warin drank outside our tent, and my family sat with him for the entirety of the opening day feast. We've only spoken around others, and then only briefly, but I've oft felt his gaze on me. I've wanted to get closer, to talk more intimately, yet I cannot forget his relationship with the queen.

He may be charming. And handsome. And clearly a man of influence. But he is not mine. And I shall never be with a man whose heart belongs to another.

Erik's axe lands in the center of the painted circle. The poor tree never stood a chance.

I gasp. "Did he win? How can he throw the axe that far so accurately?"

Warin watches me but does not answer.

"Why are you looking at me thus?"

Not for the first time, I feel as if something is amiss. Warin, in particular, has been behaving oddly.

"You like him?" His words sound more like an accusation than a question.

"I hardly know him," I counter.

"You did once."

"That was many, many years ago."

Cheers break out, interrupting our conversation. Erik speaks to the constable and then seems to glance our way.

"Aye," Warin says, standing, "he has won. And I believe he wishes to speak to you."

Sure enough, Erik is walking toward us. Without his surcoat, he looks less like a commander and more like a Highlander today. Leather boots, breeches, and a loose linen shirt, its ties hanging open at his chest. I cannot take my eyes off him.

I get up so quickly I almost trip.

"'I hardly know him,'" Warin mocks as he assists me down the stands. I don't have time to shush him before Erik reaches us.

"Well done," I offer, dropping the skirts I'd lifted to descend the steps. As spectators stream past us, we move off to the side of the field.

"Rawlins seems pleased," my brother comments to Erik. And, indeed, his opponent is staring at us with obvious contempt. I look away quickly.

Erik huffs a laugh. "He is a traitorous backstabber who did not deserve to regain his lands."

I look between Erik and my brother, attempting to pretend the former is just an acquaintance. Truthfully, I've never dreamed of kissing any of my acquaintances . . . or any man, until this morn. Not even Sir Edward, the only man I've actually kissed. My parents hinted at a possible match between the border lord and me, and he visited us at Blackwell on his way to the coast. When he approached me in the garden one day, I decided not to decline his offer of a kiss.

Handsome, though not nearly as so as Erik, Sir Edward was also extremely courteous. But that kiss . . . it was nothing like the tales my sister was so fond of reading about, kisses so wondrous they made men, and women, do reckless things.

Before Fara died, I didn't think to marry for love. I expected to be matched with someone who might strengthen Moray alliances. But my sister dreamed of a match like our parents' marriage, and after she died, I started to imagine what Fara would have said about each of my suitors. This one was a bore. That one would never let me alone. Another would not allow me an opinion.

49

I still wait for the day Father's patience will run out, and I will be told to marry. But, thankfully, it did not happen with Sir Edward.

"We bore your sister with talk of Rawlins and the match."

I realize both men are looking at me. They're so in sync it's hard to remember our fathers now despise each other. I'm glad for it. Their quarrel needn't be ours.

"As champion of the Triumph," Erik says, "I've been invited to Havefest."

Havefest. I've heard of the celebration, of course. Father has attended it more than once. Aside from it being held out of doors with a small, exclusive guest list, I know little else.

Erik and Warin exchange a look.

"Would you join me, Lady Reyne?"

It is as if I am suddenly aware of every sound, every movement around us. I inhale deeply, attempting not to attract undue notice.

"You are allowed a guest?" My voice sounds so calm. *Well done, Reyne.*

He glances at Warin.

"One, aye."

That means . . .

"Will your companion not be sorry to miss it?"

His answer is swift. "Nay."

"My father will be there as well? As a past champion?"

Again, my brother gives him *that look*. I will ask Warin about it the moment Erik leaves, for I'm now convinced he's hiding something . . . something to do with Erik.

"I believe he will, but I would escort you there as my guest."

"I would be delighted."

"Very good," he says, a bit formally. "I shall ask your father's permission and see you at your tents this eve."

Bowing, he returns to the constable and a few others who have been waiting to speak to him.

"I've never been to Havefest," Warin comments. "Imagine, this is your first tourney, and you'll be attending the most coveted event of all."

We walk toward the field where Warin will compete next in the hammer throw. Shouts erupt to our left, though from this distance I cannot see precisely which event is unfolding there.

"Do you believe Father will approve?"

Warin stops and looks at me.

"Warin? Tell me."

When he doesn't answer, I remind him, "Do you remember the day when you and Fara snuck into the dungeons?"

Though they've not been used for many years, Blackwell still has dungeons. My brother had a particular fascination with them, despite being told to stay away. It was only when my sister conspired to go down there with him that he was finally punished for it.

The shadow that crosses his face is quickly replaced by a sad smile.

"Aye," he says.

"I knew before you confessed. How? Because you are my brother. I can sense it now as I did then. You are hiding something from me."

Warin's next act is odder still. He takes my hands.

Though he loves me, my brother is not particularly affectionate. Of the three of us, Fara was the warmest. Always hugging, even when decorum was required. She was like Mother in that way, whereas Warin and I are more like our father.

"I love you, Reyne. Know that, above all."

"You're acting strangely, Warin, and I would know the reason."

He glances over my shoulder, then squeezes my hands and releases them.

"Walk with me this way," he says, his tone a little strained now. "Quickly."

I do as he asks, but he's mistaken if he believes I'll allow him to change the subject so easily.

"What was that . . . ?"

Warin shakes his head. "Later. Look in the direction of the market."

I do as he asks, finally understanding. Someone is behind us, someone whose conversation Warin wishes to overhear. He points as if explaining something to me but says nothing.

I do not know who stands behind us, but I can hear their words clearly. Both are men, their voices unfamiliar.

"Before the melee," one says.

"He will be there?" his companion replies.

"Aye."

"Is it not risky, coming here?"

"Not as risky as inaction. Now is the time to strike."

The men grow quiet. And then, the voices are gone.

"Come. We must talk to Father," Warin says, turning about and walking toward the lists. There's no sign of the men whose conversation we overheard. I try to look for them, but Warin stops me.

"Don't look. I think they grew suspicious."

My brother is fairly running now.

"They?"

As we continue moving forward, hustling at an uncomfortable pace, Warin explains.

"One of those men was with Lord Rawlins earlier, just before the Triumph. They looked suspicious enough that I sent my page to listen to their conversation."

"Do you make a practice of eavesdropping?"

Warin rolls his eyes at me. "You know I do not. But Rawlins cannot be trusted. Father does not like or trust the man. He's both Borderer and Highlander, and some resent him for attempting to be both."

Something I've never quite been able to understand.

"Are we not all one? Meria is the enemy, aye? Why must we fight each other?"

I lift my skirts as Warin increases his pace.

"We've different interests. Borderers would have us fighting always with Meria."

A fact I know well, for they are constantly trying to pull Father into their battles.

"They accuse us of lending support to Meria by our inaction."

"I know all of this," I charge. "Even still, we are one. We must find common ground or risk being made weaker against Meria."

Warin smiles. "Spoken like a Moray. But this time, I fear things are different. The Borderers are not alone in their thirst for war. After the failed attack of the Oryan, some of the Highland lords are calling for war too."

I know they are the enemy, but still I cannot help but feel for the men who sank with that ship. One moment, they rode atop the water, safe and secure, and the next they were being pulled into it, compelled by a force so strong that it felled two hundred of Meria's best warriors.

Just like it did my poor, innocent, Fara.

"Reyne?"

My pace had slowed, my mind caught up in its dark, cycling thoughts.

"Apologies," I say. "So what does all of this mean? Who is the 'he' they spoke of?"

53

"I'm uncertain. But the page reported something quite interesting."

We're approaching the lists now, and I see Father in the distance, practicing for one of the events he has chosen to enter this year. Though he no longer participates in the melee, he still can toss a poleaxe farther than anyone and is preparing to show as much.

What will he say to Erik about this eve?

But I force myself to ask a different question of my brother. "What did he report?"

My brother does not slow down, prompting odd looks from those closest to us.

"Rawlins told him, 'The time has come. Another Saitford is necessary.'"

Allowing Warin to rush toward our father, I stop completely.

Another Saitford.

The attack that saw half a village slaughtered, women and children among them.

None know who did it, just that the perpetrators were seen crossing the border back to Edingham. Some said the Borderers were responsible. Others blamed the queen herself. Still other rumors named the Shadow Warriors, as they are the only force of men known for their ability to blend into the landscape, unseen, and those who attacked the village of Saitford disappeared.

It was that attack that prompted King Galfrid to send a ship full of men to our shores.

Another Saitford?

I watch as Warin reaches my father. What plot has my brother stumbled on? And who was coming here, to Leden-hill, on the morning of the melee? And then there was Warin's peculiar behavior before we witnessed the conversation. He's only professed his love to me a handful of times before. Why now?

What did it all mean?

If such intrigue is customary at the Tournament of Loigh, it is no wonder my father nearly missed my sister's birth to attend it.

9

ERIK

I navigate the sea of tents, proof that I'm not the only one who failed to take our host up on his offer to stay within the castle walls. Normally, such an offer would be welcome at a tournament. Men like Moray would be staying inside Ledenhill Castle too. But this tourney is different, its purpose to solidify the unofficial Highland oath, that the Mountain Men, as they were called years ago, swear allegiance first and foremost to each other. It is an opportunity to reconnect. To strengthen allegiances. Those who stay within the castle walls were met with suspicion.

I round the corner and ride toward Moray's tents. He and Warin sit around a fire with at least six other men. But there's no sign of Reyne.

Before I can approach, Warin stands and rushes toward me. At first, I think he means to revoke his permission for me to escort Reyne tonight. Something I've looked forward to all day. But something else flashes in his eyes.

"I'd speak to you before you leave."

He pulls me off to the side even as I make eye contact with Moray, who does not appear to be dressed for the feast.

"Do you know a man by the name of Edward Kyle?"

I think for a moment before shaking my head. "I've never heard of him."

"I'm going to tell you something, Stokerton, as you're courting my sister. And because I know you to be a good and honorable man. But if our paths should not converge, you must vow to pursue this matter using the connections available to you."

"It would be easier to make such a vow if I knew of what we discuss?"

He glances at the smaller tent to the left of the one where Moray and I first met. I know it is Reyne's and that she's likely inside with her handmaiden, preparing.

"She will be out any moment," Warin confirms.

His behavior is slightly alarming. From what I remember of the boy, Warin was much like his father. As stoic as I am not. A trait I could admire though am unable to emulate. But this eve he is anything but.

"Go on," I say, unwilling to fully commit to him until I know more.

"Earlier today I spied a man, apparently his name is Edward Kyle, the third son of a minor Borderland family, speaking with Rawlins. It seemed suspicious enough that I sent a page to listen to their conversation. Rawlins told him, 'Another Saitford is necessary.' I saw the man again later, speaking with someone I do not know. Reyne and I were able to listen to enough of their conversation to learn something will occur the morning of the melee while everyone is distracted. Kyle said, 'He will be there' and that 'now is the time to strike.'"

Becoming more and more alarmed as Warin speaks, I attempt to put all of this information together.

"Who will be there? And what is happening the morning of the melee?"

He gives me a flat stare. Of course he does not know the answer to either question. But Warin is correct about one thing. This matter must be pursued.

"When Rawlins said another Saitford was necessary, my stomach turned, knowing what happened in that village. Knowing it was our own countrymen who did such a thing," Warin says.

Could Lord Rawlins be personally responsible for the attack?

I consider what I know about the man. His land lies at the foot of the Loigh Mountains. Hempswood Castle was one of the first built here in Edingham, but it has changed hands many times, moving back and forth between Rawlins and the Merians. Most recently, Rawlins took it back with the help of mercenaries at a considerable loss.

"How long ago did Rawlins regain Hempswood?"

Warin frowns. "My father remembers the battle well and says it was nearly ten years ago."

"What would he have to gain were Cettina to agree to an attack on Meria?" I ask, not expecting a response. The meaning is clear to both of us—if Rawlins did such a thing, his intention was to provoke the queen to attack Meria. And, since it did not work, he aims to do it again to force her hand.

A stillness descends around us, prompting me to turn toward the tents.

I can no longer move or talk, struck dumb by the sight of Reyne in the deepest of royal blue dresses, its sleeves nearly down to the floor, her hair free-flowing with not one adornment . . . she is magnificent.

I want her.

Not for the allegiance her father brings. But for her. I want her against me, her lips pressed on mine.

"I've not seen you look so serious before," she says to me as Warin and I rejoin the others at the fire.

"This is a serious occasion," I respond. "A first for us both."

"Father"—she leans down to kiss him on the cheek —"thank you."

Apparently he has decided to allow me to escort her alone? Does she not think such a thing strange? He doesn't appear at all guilty for accepting the thanks of the daughter he'd deceived, however well-intentioned the deception. Warin, on the other hand, looks as if he might be ill. Because of what he learned? Or because his sister knows nothing of our plan?

"I will return her safely," I vow. "You have my word."

Warin levels a stern gaze at me. "We will take you at it."

As the others gathered around the fire go back to their conversation, I offer my arm to Reyne. She tucks her hands into it, and together we move toward the horses.

"Will you ride with me?"

She looks at a beautiful white mare, considering, and then back to me.

"Aye."

Though at first I'm glad for her agreement, we're not far away from the tents before I begin to regret the offer. Reyne fits snugly in front of me, her hair just inches from my nose, the scent of roses particularly pleasant compared to the stench I've been subjected to all day: men who've not bathed in days despite participating in various events.

One of the oddities at the capital is that baths are regular occurrences, and it's something I've become accustomed to. I'm unsure how Reyne manages to smell so sweet.

"I am a bit nervous," she says, turning back toward me. In the growing darkness, I cannot see her freckles.

"This is really nothing more than an out of doors feast."

She looks to the left of us, away from the castle.

In truth, I am nervous too, but the problem of Rawlins's cryptic meeting and the possibility of an impending disaster cannot be solved this night. I vow to put it out of my mind and concentrate on winning the hand of the woman I've now resolved to make my own.

She doesn't answer. There is nothing to the left of us save the woods and a vast stretch of marshland beyond it. Up ahead, the castle and its many torchlights. Behind us and to the right, the fields and tents from which we just came.

"Reyne?"

She doesn't answer.

"What is out here that worries you so?"

She turns away from me so that I cannot see her face any longer. A pity.

"The stream."

The stream?

"'Tis that way, is it not?" she presses.

"Aye."

I do not understand. Until I do.

Fear is as irrational as it is powerful. It is a lesson I've had occasion to learn.

"We will be nowhere near it. That stream cannot hurt you. Do you understand? You are safe, Reyne."

"I am, aye. 'Tis such a silly thing."

I pull on the reins, stopping us completely. When she turns back toward me, I resist the urge to kiss her as a way to appease her fear.

"It is not a silly thing. You were there when she drowned, weren't you?" I guess.

"Aye."

"There is nothing more painful than watching someone die, especially someone you love."

Or someone you had a direct hand in killing. Unfortunately, I know what that is like from experience.

"That pain will never go away," I say, as much to her as myself. "But you will learn to live with it, and to think of your sister without guilt."

Her eyes widen.

"I will not tell you 'twas not your fault, because you will likely never believe me. But I will tell you this, Reyne. Someday you will stand along a riverbank without fear."

She shakes her head, but I saw the look in her eyes. I know why she hasn't come to this tournament before. Why she seems less carefree than the girl I once knew. Why the light within her has dimmed.

"Nay," she says, not believing me. But she does not have to. I can believe in her enough for us both.

REYNE

*W*hen Erik suggested we ride together, I could not think of a reason to say nay. I knew there was a stream beyond the castle. My father had readily agreed to enter the castle grounds from the west gate, farther away, but I didn't feel comfortable telling Erik to do so. If I'd been on my own horse . . . but I wasn't, and I found it impossible to admit my fear to him.

I should have expected Erik to react the way he did. A perfect knight, his manners refined from years at court, he knew precisely what to say. When we were children, I cannot say Erik Stokerton and I were friends, precisely. I saw him few times, and much of his visits he spent with my brother.

Now, as he gives the groom the horse's reins, I'm sorry our fathers stopped speaking. Perhaps we could have been true friends.

Although the look he gives me now, the same one he graced me with as I came out of the tent, is not that of a friend. I find myself responding, my finger itching to push the lock of hair falling into his eye back into place. A fortnight ago, I wished only to learn how to live in the world without my sister. A sennight ago, I could think only of the journey here, the peril of crossing two rivers and coming closer to the water than I had since losing Fara.

These last two days, my thoughts have been more and more focused on the man offering his arm to me. And while it is a pleasant distraction, it is also a fleeting one. But does that mean I cannot enjoy it while it lasts?

"Good eve, my lord, my lady."

We are hardly beyond the stables when an older man with kind eyes approaches us.

"I am the seneschal of Ledenhill Castle. As you know, Havefest is held out of doors. If you will walk that path, to the right of the keep, you'll find your way to the small courtyard."

A seneschal greeting us here is quite unusual. But then, my father warned me this night will be unlike any other feast I've ever attended. Erik and I exchange a glance, our arms tucked together. He smells musky, entirely pleasant, which I cannot say about some of the men we've journeyed with.

I realize I'm staring.

"Have you ever been greeted at the stables by a seneschal before?" I ask.

"Nay, I've not. But then this is my first Havefest, so I am prepared for anything."

As we make our way up the cobblestone path, servants and other castle inhabitants watch us walk by. I feel very much on display, but also . . . content.

And something else I cannot name.

"Do you hear it?"

I do now. Music in the distance, up ahead.

"I am surprised you've not been to Havefest before."

And then I realize the high compliment I've paid him. Only Triumph champions, those who have hosted the Tournament of Loigh in the past, the leaders of the melee, and the proclaimed champion of the winning side are invited to attend this event. Few men indeed.

"This is just my third time attending the tourney," he says, "and only once did I participate in the melee."

That surprises me.

"My father and brother attend every year," I say.

The music becomes louder as we approach.

"After the Battle of Hendrelds Hill, my father became more distant. More of a Highlander, if such a thing is possible."

I understand his meaning. We're known for staying close to home. Traveling little, trusting few. This tournament is an exception.

"But this tourney?" I say. "My father says it is a reminder of Edingham's foundation. The Tree of Loigh a symbol of new beginnings."

"It is all of that. But . . ."

We slow down, now alone between the keep and another stone structure, mayhap the bakery or the kitchens? The music in the distance is louder now, and glowing torches line the pathway.

"That tree is not the same symbol for all," he finishes.

I am very much aware that Erik still holds my arm, though he loosens his grip just a bit to turn toward me.

"What do you mean?" Though a part of me is curious about what lies ahead, I cannot imagine it will be more magical than this moment, with this man.

He holds my gaze as he speaks. "To some, it is a symbol of freedom. When King Onry named Aiden's twin as successor, those who followed him over the mountains called Aiden valiant and adventurous for rejecting his father's decision and leaving court. Unafraid of the repercussions of his actions, which later led to Meria splitting into two."

This is precisely what my father believes.

"Others call Aiden disloyal. For disobeying his father, abandoning his brother, and weakening the Isle. They see the Tree of Loigh as a source of evil and ill-gotten gains at the expense of the whole of the Isle."

"Merians believe this." I know it already.

"Nay." Erik shakes his head. "Not only Merians. But others loyal to Edingham and the Borea line."

Was he saying . . . ?

"Do you believe it so?"

Erik doesn't answer. Instead, he asks, "Most important are not my beliefs, or your parents' or your brother's. What do *you* believe?"

I blink. "I believe . . . I do not know? None have asked me that question before."

His smile is like a thousand May Days in one afternoon.

"Give it some thought," he says, "but not this eve. Havefest is not for politics." His smile falters, just a bit. "Even if the world weighs heavily on us just now."

His words prompt us to begin walking again, but he hasn't finished. Stealing a look at me, he says, "It is for celebrating. Enjoying life and every one of its pleasures."

A pleasurable shiver runs through me.

"Look."

As we round the corner, I cannot help but do so. A small courtyard, small by this castle's standards at least, is lit by torch after torch, candle after candle. Not only from the usual places but from seemingly everywhere.

And the flowers! Some are familiar to me, but others . . . they are everywhere.

In the center of it all, a fire. Not like the small campfires back at the tents, but the largest fire I've ever seen, contained in the middle of the courtyard behind the main keep. Great lords stand about, their wives dressed as finely as if they were at court, the latest fashions, like sleeves down to the ground, evident.

"How does everything not catch aflame?"

The light and heat of it beckons as we walk forward.

"By respecting it." Erik looks at me as if he wants to say more.

An odd answer, to be sure, but an interesting one too.

A maid approaches us with a silver tray. "Wine, my lord? My lady?"

I wait for Erik to take the goblets, but instead he looks at me.

"She serves both red and white. What is your preference?"

My preference is to be asked which wine I would like or my thoughts on politics. The only decision of importance I've ever made at Blackwell is the choice of a husband. A decision, I will admit, most in my station do not have.

But most decisions are made without consulting me, and no one has ever asked for my opinion about politics. I find it to my liking.

"Red wine, if you please."

He takes two goblets from the tray, thanking her.

"You are very polite," I say.

Meeting my eyes, he clinks his goblet to mine. "You are very beautiful."

I'd been about to take a sip when he says it. I am not practiced enough to pretend his words don't affect me.

But I have been taught enough to know one thing. Always, always accept a compliment. Without qualifying it.

"Many thanks." I lift my drink once more. "And thank you for bringing me here this eve."

We stroll around the fire, and though I do not recognize anyone, Erik either knows most of the men here, or they speak to him because he is the queen's commander. We find our hosts, and only after speaking to them do I realize . . .

"There are no trestle tables."

Instead, food is carried on trays. I've accepted fruits and small meat pies, so small they fit on two fingers. We watch dancers and jugglers as the audience of less than thirty people talks and laughs.

"Do you have feasts such as this at the capital?"

We stand not far from the fire, surrounded by festivities yet still quite alone.

"Of this sort? Nay. Though I shall speak to the queen about starting such a tradition."

His words remind me of one of many reasons this current obsession with Lord Erik Stokerton, the queen's commander, cannot stand.

"Tell me of her." I am curious, despite his ties to her.

"The queen?"

"Aye."

He takes a sip of wine, and I do the same.

"She is unlike her father in every way. He was quick to anger, she is even-tempered. King Malcom curried favor with those most loyal by promising that which he could not, or should not, deliver. Cettina does it by respecting those around her and asking their opinion. Malcom would have considered that weak. But the queen does not believe relying on others is weak at all, and that is her strength. She is firm but kind."

If I had wondered about the truthfulness of the rumors before, Erik has just answered the question for me. Cettina, he calls her. And he speaks of her as if she were a goddess, not quite human.

"You care for her?"

The words fly from my mouth, and I wish to stuff them back.

He is offended. Rightly so.

Erik sighs. "You've heard rumors, then?"

I don't wish to answer, but it seems I must.

Nodding, I take a long sip from my goblet so I can avoid speaking.

"Do not believe all of what you hear, Reyne. There are those in the capital who spew untruths as if they are facts, for their own purposes."

Is he denying it, then? But Erik did not actually say nay, he does not love the queen.

"I do not have the opportunity to hear much," I admit. "But 'tis my own doing."

A new song begins, and a tray of pastries are presented to us.

I've never attended a feast where all courses were combined. Of course, I've also never attended one without tables. In a courtyard.

"The water holds you back?" he guesses.

"Aye."

Part of me wishes to say more, but most of me does not.

"But I am here now. And as you say, this night is about enjoying life and all it offers us."

Erik looks at me in a way that makes my core clench.

"Its pleasures, I believe I said."

I swallow. "Aye." I lift my goblet. "Such as good wine. Sindridge, I believe."

Our feud with Meria has a long history, but none on the Isle have ever stopped trading with wine merchants from Sindridge. Sometimes I think it is the only reason we've gone so long without declaring all-out war on Meria.

His smile broadens.

"And music." I nod toward the musicians. "The pipers are most talented."

The corners of Erik's eyes wrinkle, but still I cannot stop myself.

"And of course the entertainment. Who do you believe will follow the jugglers?"

He does not answer.

Instead, he moves even closer to me. So close I can smell his unique scent once again.

"Those are all most enjoyable, but . . . there are pleasures you seem to be forgetting about, Reyne."

Oh dear.

"The food?" I venture.

His laugh is deep and all-encompassing, and I have the strange fancy that I'd like to drape it all over me.

"Those are not precisely the pleasures I referred to."

Don't ask. Don't ask.

"So which ones do you mean?"

I asked.

And I fear Erik is about to answer.

11

ERIK

I have seduced women before, so I know this is the very moment I should continue to pursue Reyne. If I willed it, and I most certainly do, I'd taste those sweet lips even before the night is through.

And yet, the deception weighs heavily on me.

'Tis for Cettina. For Edingham. And you want her. Badly.

Still, my mother's words the night before I left for the court ring in my ears.

"Do not let them change you, son."

They have tried. At times, unintentionally—the customs there just different than in the Highlands—and other times much more pointedly. Many have tried to bribe me for the queen's ear.

But I am the son of Bern Stokerton. Proud Highlander and a good man. Equally important, I am the son of Lady Mariam, great-granddaughter of one of the greatest Legion of Ash members who ever existed. And though the legion is no more, the particular ways of those warriors fading, their vows were not only instilled in their members, but in their families as well.

No price is worth the loss of *integritatem*. Once lost, it cannot be bought back.

"I would speak to you, Reyne."

Those words might very well mean doom for Edingham. Without the Highlanders' support, Cettina is convinced her will may not be enough to avoid a war.

"Are we not talking now?"

I look around the courtyard. None of the other guests seem to pay us any mind. And no wonder. The fire burns high and bright. The food and music and wine have lulled our companions into a state of contentment.

"Come."

We make our way around the fire, and I lead her down the cobblestone walkway, less well-lit than the main path, to a seated alcove.

"How did you know this was here?"

"I've been trained to notice things," I say, holding out my hand and gesturing toward the velvet cushions that had likely been placed on the stone seats for this very event.

I sit across from her, a torch from an embrasure above illuminating Reyne's untamed red hair as she moves it back over her shoulders.

She's grown so lovely. Into a woman I'd gladly take as my wife, a possibility that will become much less likely after this conversation.

Reyne does not sit.

Instead, she makes to move past me but stops so close we could be touching.

"Would you like to sit?" I ask. "We must talk, Reyne."

Her lips open so slightly I might have missed it were it not for the torchlight above us. We are close enough to hear the music in the courtyard, but these are not joyful pipes. Instead, a harpist begins to play. The haunting sounds give the moment a much more poignant feel, as if . . .

As if it means to bring us together.

She wants you to kiss her.

Reyne will want no such thing in a moment. I am almost uncourtly enough to take advantage of the situation, driven by the thoughts of kissing her that have swirled through my head from the moment I saw her outside that tent. The last thing I wanted before this journey was a wife. That I did not recoil from the idea can be ascribed to the very pleasing notion of being joined to this woman whose lips are mere inches from mine.

I can almost feel the taste of her already.

But if we kiss . . .

If we kiss, our path is set. Until the moment, a fortnight from now, when she learns I've been deceiving her. If I wait so long, it is likely she will refuse to marry me then, so what am I really risking now?

Damn Moray.

"Please," I say, instead of pulling her toward me and taking that which we both want. "We must talk."

Rather than wait for her to do so, I uncourteously sit before she does. I need to put distance between us. The look of disappointment on her face is such that I drink deeply from the goblet I still carry, wishing I'd taken more before we found this lovers' corner.

Shifting on the soft velvet cushion, I take a deep breath and attempt to remind my wayward body there'll be no kissing tonight. Not only will I not taste those luscious lips, I'll be quite lucky if Reyne allows me to escort her back to the tents.

Where do I begin?

"I'm sorry, Reyne."

Again, before the words spill from my mouth, I wonder if this is the right decision. If Lord Rawlins truly was behind the attack on Saitford, and is now planning another such onslaught, my mission here has shifted from gaining the support of Moray and the Highland lords to uncovering and stopping a potential plot.

Or both.

I know what Cettina would have me do. But I cannot lie to this woman any longer.

"After the attack on Saitford," I say. Reyne's brows furrow at the sudden change in topic, but I press on. ". . . the call for a counter-attack on Meria was immediate. However, Cettina is not convinced it is the best course for Edingham, an assessment I agree with even more now, having learned what we did earlier today."

"Why are you telling me this?"

A fair question.

"Whereas her father would have mounted an attack already, Cettina sent a contingent to King Galfrid to open a discussion. A move which infuriated some in the capital and beyond it."

Reyne waits patiently for me to continue.

"The calls for war grow louder, even among the Highland lords, who typically avoid the politics of Edingham. Cettina's allies cannot quell them all. Only your father would be able to do so effectively."

I can see she begins to understand, but unfortunately, I'm not yet finished with my tale. Bracing myself for her anger, I continue.

"I was sent here to gain his support. To ask for his assistance in helping Cettina calm the Highlanders."

Reyne laughs. "Then your visit here is for naught. Since Hendrelds, he has withdrawn his involvement with the crown in all matters. If your queen attempts to tame him, I wish her well. It cannot be done."

I sigh, understanding Moray's position, unwilling to remind Reyne, or her father, they are still subjects of the crown. But I know such a reminder would only serve to inflame matters, especially if it came from the son of Bern Stokerton.

This is the reason, I've always believed, I was made commander. A Highlander myself, I understand what those who were not raised in these mountains do not. In all but name, these men and women are as independent as those in Murwood End.

"She does not wish to tame him, but to work with him to avoid a war. One which may even make its way into the mountains."

Reyne, still amused, speaks like a Moray. "With a king wrapped up in a battle over his own succession? Who just lost two hundred of his best men? I think not, Erik. If war comes to Edingham, it will come to its border and its shores. Not the Highlands."

I do not wish to be harsh, but I will be nonetheless.

"We've taken children within the castle walls who lost both their mother and their father at Saitford. One who lost an ear and another who was carried through the gates by a farmer whose land was burned. The lad was still covered in his mother's blood."

Reyne recoils at my words.

"I serve all of Edingham."

Her demeanor has changed, understandably. This is not how I wished this conversation to begin, but mayhap it is the way it needs to go. A shame, as the light above us, the music behind us, and the free-flowing wine could have made this a very different evening. But there is no time for fanciful notions.

Not for me. Not for Edingham.

"And so I came here, to this tourney, to speak to your father."

Reyne raises her chin. "And you've done so. What did he

say?"

I do not mince words.

"That he would not give his support." Her nod says she expected as such, but I press on. "Unless he counts me as son-in-law. Then, and only then, will he give me his support."

It takes her a moment, but when she understands, Reyne shoots up. I stand as well, reaching out a calming hand and laying it on her shoulder. She will not be pacified.

"He . . . he has no right," she seethes.

Although we both know that he does.

"Why would he do such a thing?" Reyne shoves my hand from her, so I back away. Neither of us sit down. I attempt to take the goblet from her hand, as it tilts precariously to the left, but she pulls it away.

"Our lands border each other's and"—I attempt a smile —"I am not a monster, Reyne. Your father knows me as well as any man."

Her shoulders rise and fall in anger. But at least she has not fled. Instead, she raises the jeweled goblet to her lips and drinks. Deeply. She does not stop until it is empty, at which point she does hand it to me.

Only to take my mostly full one.

Not the reaction I'd expected.

"You agreed to this?" Another sip, this time of my wine.

"I did."

Her laugh is bitter. "Of course you did. You are the queen's commander, and would do anything for"—she pauses—"Edingham."

But we both know she meant to say *the queen*.

On both accounts, she is correct.

Any attempt to charm her will not work. So I do not try. I tell her only the truth. "I agreed because I find the idea appealing." I pause, then come out with the rest of it. "He told me that you would not marry me, that you wish to marry for love."

If I wanted to make her angrier, I've accomplished the feat.

"I accepted the challenge," I say, perhaps too bluntly. "Gladly."

Her eyes pierce mine, and then she takes another sip of the wine. When she hands me the second empty goblet, I turn to place them on the ground next to the stone seat. When I pull upright to face her again, Reyne is already two steps away.

I grab her arm gently, unwilling for her to misunderstand.

"Would you have preferred for me to continue to hide the truth? In telling you, I risk any chance at gaining the Highland lords' support. We march another step toward war, which is precisely what some of our own men wish for. I risk . . ."

I let her go. I'd speak to her, make Reyne understand, but I will not keep her here against her will.

"You risk angering the queen."

I was going to say, *I risk losing you before you were even mine*. But I know she'd not believe me. While I did not come to Ledenhill for a wife, I would gladly leave here with one, if that wife were the redheaded siren in front of me.

This, I realize, is the girl I knew. The one with fire in her eyes. Lady Reyne Moray, before she lost her sister. Before life beat her down and tried to turn her meek.

"I might have done it," she says, still not turning to leave but clearly unhappy with her present company. "He will force me to marry soon enough. 'Tis my duty to do so, as it is my brother's. And you . . ." Her eyes soften, for just a moment. "Despite your deception, or perhaps because you told me of it when my father, and I am assuming my brother,

did not see it necessary to do so . . . aye, I might have done it .
. . if not for the fact that you are in love with the queen."

It is as if she punched me in the chest.

"I cannot marry a man who loves another."

With that, Reyne walks away. This time, I will not try to
stop her. For what, precisely, would I say?

REYNE

*I*t stuns me to return to the courtyard and find it as it was before my world was turned upside down. While the other guests have seemingly been enjoying the food and music, and most especially the wine, I've been learning how very little my own father and brother care for me.

So that was why Warin acted so strangely. And Father? I am less angry with him, for such a thing could almost be expected from him. Accustomed to giving orders without asking for input, he is exactly the sort of man who would conspire with another over his own daughter's future.

How many times I've wished to be a man. Or if not a man, then a woman who actually wields power. Like an abbess. A Garra.

Or even a queen.

Why I should be angry at *Cettina*, as Erik calls her, I do not know. In fact, before this tourney, I was proud to live in a kingdom ruled by a woman. And though many worry she is ill-equipped to rule, my mother insists it's a victory that she has been mostly accepted as the Isle's first queen.

Victory, indeed.

"Wine, my lady?" a servant says, coming around with a tray.

I've drunk two full goblets, rather quickly.

"Aye," I say, despite it. Taking the goblet from her, I move to a darkened corner as Erik emerges. I left him in a rage, not considering how I would return to the tents. I could walk, of course. It is far, but not so far as to be impossible. But what if I wander in the wrong direction under the cover of darkness, toward the river?

Shuddering at the thought, I sip my wine and decide to ask our host for an escort back. Of course, Erik, who is looking for me, is standing directly next to the man.

Why must he be so handsome? And kind?

And in love with the queen?

It is clear the rumors are true, and he did not even trouble himself to deny them. As I said to him, the idea of marrying a man who loves another . . . I would prefer to be wed to the doddering old fool who visited Blackwell during our May Day celebrations to ask my father to accept a union between us.

Since then, Father has broached the subject more often, but I always deflect the topic back to my brother. He is both older and the heir to Blackwell. Surely he should marry first? But nay, he is allowed to wander the Isle to discover himself while I remain in the mountains with no prospects for a husband and a father increasingly inclined to find me one.

Indeed, Erik Stokerton would have been more than acceptable.

I thought he would kiss me. And I'd have let him do it. What would it be like to kiss a man such as he? He would be well-practiced, a fact that does not exactly recommend him. But still . . .

"Do you think a woman such as you could possibly hide, Reyne?"

My shoulders sag in defeat. I turn, wondering how he managed to sneak up on me when I was looking at him just a moment ago.

"You clearly know nothing of your own appeal."

My traitorous heart flutters at his compliment. Weak. I am a weak little fool to be wooed by his honeyed words now that he's shared his true intention.

"I am not hiding." I hold up my goblet. "Merely enjoying a bit of wine."

I expect him to chastise me, as my father would surely do at such excess, but he merely smiles.

"Then I shall stand with you, enjoying . . ." He looks around, but there is no maidservant nearby. Having satisfied himself that we are alone, he turns his attention back to me. ". . . you enjoying your wine."

Oh dear. *Resist, Reyne.*

"I'd have left already." I take a sip. "But alas, I've no mount or sense of which direction our tents lie."

"I am aware."

"Though I'd have found my way."

"I am aware of that as well."

I cannot think normally when he is this near.

"Would you like me to escort you back now, Lady Reyne?"

Before I can answer that, aye, I would like that, and also, nay, I would not, the musicians stop and the lord and lady of Ledenhill hold up their hands. We move away from the bonfire toward them.

"Greetings. Have you enjoyed your evening thus far?"

A cheer rises up. I pay mind to my goblet, and not to my companion.

"You are here, past and present champions and former hosts of the Tournament of Loigh."

Father would never willingly miss such an honor. His decision to stay behind this eve shocked me, both because he has spoken highly of the event in the past and because he allowed me to be escorted alone. His behavior convinced me something was amiss, just like Warin's, although both steadfastly denied any wrongdoing.

Liars, both of them.

"We gather as a reminder of our triumph over those who would conquer us. These are games, aye, but they represent unity of the Highland way. We also welcome a special guest this eve, the queen's commander, Lord Erik Stokerton."

One by one, the guests turn toward us.

"To Queen Cettina"—the host raises his goblet—"to Edingham, and to the Mountain Men."

"And women," I mutter, drinking.

"And women," Erik repeats. "You would like her," he tells me as a maidservant hands him a new goblet. I do not need to ask of whom he speaks. It's on the tip of my tongue to tell him he's wrong, but I refrain from saying so. The musicians have struck up another song, so at least the attention is no longer so squarely on us.

So this is envy. I know the signs from "Roman de la Lily," a poem where a man falls in love with a flower.

Aye. A flower.

His friends and family become jealous of his love, and they all eventually leave him.

"A smile? The first since I ruined your evening."

I would tell Erik he did not, but I do not make it a practice of lying.

"I was thinking of 'Roman de la Lily.' It's a—"

"Poem. LaRus falls in love with a lily. He wakes each day

81

thinking of his love. Written during King Onry's reign, I believe."

"You read poetry?"

Also, why am I still speaking to him, precisely? Blast him for being so *interesting*.

"Nay, I am sorry to say I do not. But 'tis often read at court, and I remember that one for its absurd topic and how, despite being simple, it manages to address politics, medicine, gender, envy, and even religion. It was the topic of conversation for nearly a fortnight."

"That is the brilliance of it."

Laughter beside us draws our attention. The gathering becomes increasingly jovial as sweets begin to circulate. I cannot resist a sugared pear when it's offered to me. Erik takes my drink so smoothly, I hardly realize he's done so until I'm finished with the half pear.

"'Tis delicious," I say, wiping its juice from the corner of my mouth.

Erik watches me, and despite myself, I feel another flutter between my legs. When he hands back the goblet, his fingers touch mine, lingering there long enough to make me forget, albeit temporarily, that he is here only to forge an alliance with my father.

"It looks delicious."

I'd say he was speaking of the pear, but it is gone. And Erik stares directly at my mouth, looking very much like he did earlier. As if he desires me.

Which he does.

As a wife, to please his queen.

"Dance with me."

My answer is swift. I enjoy dancing, but I am quite ready to leave. And I tell Erik as much.

He does not respond at first.

"I am sorry for deceiving you, Reyne. I never thought to

involve you in this. When your father proposed a union, it came as a surprise, as you can imagine. I should have told you straightaway. I'd not want to be deceived as you were."

I hate myself for wanting to stay. To dance. To have him continue to look at me as if he wants to be here with me, and not because of my father.

For still wanting him to kiss me.

"You do not trust me. Nor should you, Reyne. But dance with me. Forgive me for just this eve. Enjoy this"—he waves his arms in the air—"and then tomorrow, you can choose never speak to me again if you so desire."

While I attempt to decide, he deftly takes my goblet once more, places it onto a wooden tray propped atop a barrel for such a purpose, and takes my hand. His grip is strong and sure, and although I know he'd free me if I pulled away, I can't lie to myself. I don't want to.

When he splays a hand on my lower back, the fingers of his other hand wrap around my hand. I've danced this way many times, but never, not once, have I felt this way. This is no simple dance.

We both sense as much, I think.

The sleeve of my dress falls, revealing the lower part of my arm. He looks at it, as if imagining what else it might reveal, then glances up at my face. Erik's eyes, hooded and piercing, so much more serious than his usual jovial look, bore into my own.

"So you enjoy poetry still."

"Aye."

"You adored your tutor, from what I recall."

"He was like a second brother to me."

"Was?"

"He left Blackwell the year after Fara died. It had become a different sort of place, for a time. Her absence weighed heavily on all. Also, Warin and I could read and write easily by then. He traveled to the Borderlands first, and then into Meria."

Although it is unusual for someone from Edingham to live across the border, and the same is true for Merians, some people travel where work takes them, either out of necessity or wanderlust, even across the Terese River, the natural border between our kingdoms.

"And I do some writing of my own," I blurt.

Erik smiles. "What do you write?"

That is something I do not wish to reveal.

"I cannot say."

"Hmmm. Cannot." He spins me around in a dramatic fashion, and some begin to stare. "Or will not?"

His hand is warm against my back. "They are watching us."

Erik leans into me and whispers into my ear. "They are watching you. You are a beautiful woman, Reyne."

Spinning me around again, he does not allow me to respond. But as the dance begins to slow, he looks me in the eyes once again.

"I have a proposal for you."

I make a sound in my throat. He laughs aloud at the most unladylike noise. I attempt to purse my lips together, as if I am still angry, but it fails.

I should be.

I want to be.

But Erik Stokerton is making it very difficult with his easy smiles and flirty behavior.

"Give me more than one eve. Give me the tournament to win your hand, with your full knowledge of what I seek."

"But I've told you . . ."

"You've told me you will not marry a man who loves another. And yet, I've not confessed to doing so. You judge me without knowing me, but I'd not begrudge you that, as

I've wronged you sorely as well. Give me these ten days. If, when the melee is over, you wish to never see me again, then you return home to Blackwell, and I shall become nothing more than a memory."

I despise how little I want that very thing.

"But if, at the end of the tourney, I've convinced you that an alliance between us would be desirable not just to our families but both of us, then we will marry."

I begin to object when he stops me.

"Marriages have been forged on much less than two neighbors joining their lands and two people who very clearly desire each other."

Desire each other. Do I desire Erik Stokerton?

It is foolish of me to even pose the question. None other has affected me this way. And maybe he desires me as well. The look he's giving me now says he does.

But can I really marry a man who pines for another?

Many noblewomen do, and few are given the luxury of a choice. But would it not be less painful to marry a man I do not desire than to marry one I do who desires another?

"I am not asking for you to pledge your troth to me this very eve, Reyne. Ten days. And then, if you wish it, I will be gone."

I am about to answer when we are interrupted.

"Commander Stokerton?"

The man who interrupted our dance is tall, even taller than Erik. But he is not built like Erik. This man is thin. And very clearly drunk.

"You do not remember me," he says with the thick accent of a Highlander who spends little time at court. "But I remember you. Your betrothed was my niece."

13

REYNE

*Y*our betrothed was my niece.

For once, my headaches have come in handy. As the men play their games in the tourney, I sit outside the tent watching the squires and pages tidy up their masters' belongings.

Instead of confronting my father and brother, I begged their leave to remain out here to think. Still unsure what to do after last evening's revelations, I wish I were back home to ask my mother for guidance.

But then, I already know what she would say. Marry him. It is your duty to this family, and he is a good man. And I might have listened to her once. But then I think of my beautiful sister, so full of love and life. Our tutor, Ciaran, gave Fara a book once, when she was but a young girl of ten and three. *La flamme et la fleur.* It was a long poem, really. But Fara was a romantic—that's what Ciaran called her—and the old text confirmed her beliefs.

Love, she said, *was all there was in life.*

She filled her head with teachings of Garra, fascinated by their customs and beliefs and the idea that healers roamed the Isle with the sole purpose of treating ailments of the heart. She loved to debate the "great question," as it had come to be known.

Was Athea, the original Garra, responsible for the division between Meria and Edingham? After all, had she not given Lady Edina a love potion, making King Onry fall in love with her, he would have married his original betrothed. They would not have begotten two sons, twins, and have then had to choose which would sit on the throne. Sir Aiden would not have fled to the Loigh Mountains with his followers.

We would all be Merians, and Edingham would not exist. And none, not even the most independent among us, could argue we were stronger divided than we would be as one people.

When she was alive, I told Fara the tales she so loved, *La flamme et la fleur* and others like it that Ciaran found for her, were nothing more than that. Tales. Life was not so romantic as that. Noblewomen like us typically married for advantage. Land or power. To increase social standing. It was why our family had amassed the greatest force of men in the Highlands. Why Father was so respected. Years of alliances, some of which my stubborn father later broke, for dignity and honor, he would say.

But now she was gone. Her fanciful notions have become my own, for Fara is not here to live them. She believed love was everything, the start and end to life, and so I feel the need to honor that, *her*.

"Lady Reyne?"

A young man I do not know approaches, but from his clothing, I can guess his identity easily enough. I stand.

"Bradyn?" I guess. Erik told me of his squire.

He seems pleased I guessed his name.

87

"Aye, my lady. Squire to Lord Erik Stokerton, the queen's second commander," he says proudly, chin raised.

And then he says no more, so I fill the silence. "I am pleased to meet you."

He smiles and nods but says nothing. The poor boy seems nervous.

"Would you like to sit?" I offer.

He shakes his head.

"I was sent here by Lord Stokerton to give you a message."

Again, I wait. His face contours in anguish, making me want to pull him into an embrace. The poor lad is so young. And as Erik told me, without parents. A fate I'd not wish on anyone.

My father might lie and withhold information, but I would not part with him for all the world.

"I—" he stammers, "when my lord gave me the missive, I was polishing his armor, and I . . ."

He doesn't remember the message.

"Please sit," I tell him, gesturing toward my brother's empty chair in front of the tent. The boy does, and I resume my seat as well.

"Are you enjoying the tournament?"

He nods, most enthusiastically. "Aye, my lady. Very much. I've seen so many splendid things since coming into my lord's service. Breywood Castle and the East Sea. I'd never seen the sea before. I lived on a farm. But my parents were killed. I snuck onto a clothier's wagon, and Lord Stokerton made me his squire the very day we rolled into the court-yard. I was worried I'd be tossed into the dungeons but . . . I'd heard of Queen Cettina's kindness. Well, some say she is kind. Others are afraid of her. But I am not." He scrunches his nose. "Well, mayhap a bit. But she is kind too. As is my lord."

Smiling, I say a silent prayer of thanks Bradyn found his way to Erik.

"He is quite kind," I say, attempting to quell his fears about forgetting the message from Erik. A man more filled with secrets than my own father. He spoke of honesty, and yet he didn't see fit to tell me he'd been betrothed before. After the stranger's insertion into our conversation, Erik told me about his ill-fated betrothal to one of Queen Cettina's ladies. Something inside of me burned in an unfamiliar way. And yet . . . it is hard to hold a grudge against him in the face of his kindness to this boy. "Did you know I knew him when he was a young lad, like you?"

His eyes widen. "I did not."

"Lord Stokerton's land borders ours. On one occasion, I accompanied my father to a meeting and saw Erik in the courtyard, surrounded by younger children. He was acting out the story of Aiden's crossing of the Terese River."

"Before this was Edingham?"

"Aye," I say, "Lord Stokerton has always cared for others, and he will care for you well, I do believe."

I try to ignore Bradyn's suddenly glossy eyes, but my own cheeks begin to tingle. If I were to cry in front of him, surely it would summon his tears, so I push away thoughts of love and loss. Though I do believe it silly, the idea that boys or men should not cry, I know he wouldn't wish to do so in front of me.

"I remembered my lord's message," he says suddenly, bolting up from his seat as the smell of smoke reaches us. At least one fire is still burning.

"He asks that you join him for supper this eve. His tent is so large he eats in it," Bradyn exclaims. "My lord also bade me to tell you that he begs your forgiveness."

After the dual revelations of last eve, I am not surprised.

When we parted, I told him I would think on it, his request to court me at this tourney.

Which I've done.

Unfortunately, no clarity has come to me just yet. I both wish to know Erik and wish to go back home to the safety of Blackwell Castle, where there is no opportunity for my heart to be broken. Again.

'Tis just supper, nothing more.

"Please tell your lord I will have Warin escort me there at sundown."

Bradyn beams as if his mission has been successful. Pleasing him is as good a reason as any to sup with Erik this eve. The boy clearly needs encouragement after what he's been through.

"Very good, my lady. I shall tell him. My lord will be quite pleased, methinks."

His bow is so formal, I cannot help but smile.

"Good day, Lady Reyne."

"Good day, Sir Bradyn."

He frowns. "I am not yet knighted, my lady."

I make a sound of dismissal. "But you surely will be soon. Best you become accustomed to the title."

Bradyn's broad smile makes my heart so very happy. I tell myself the flutters in my middle have naught to do with the thought of supping in Erik's tent, alone with him, this eve. If Father allows it, which, given his deception, I do believe he will.

Perhaps I will not tell my father or brother that I know of their design.

This may turn out to be quite fun.

14

ERIK

"*I*'m not a goddamn maid, Erik."

For all of Gille's grumblings, he and Bradyn did well. When the idea of hosting Reyne for dinner occurred to me, I became grateful for Gille's insistence on luxuries I would never have brought with me. The table and chairs offer a place for us to eat. Bradyn found and polished the forks and knives and even rolled up the bedrolls, making it a space almost fit for a king. Or queen.

Or Reyne.

"Put them there," I say of the goblets he's procured.

After spending the entire day in this very tent, discussing the plot that seems to be unfolding even now, at this very tournament, my friend is understandably ornery.

"Take Bradyn around camp," I say. "Introduce him to the Highlanders. Maybe you will hear something."

We've agreed this is our best course. To find out what Rawlins is planning, we must both discover the location of the secret meeting and learn who of importance will be attending. Speaking to Rawlins directly would not do. His mistrust of the crown, and therefore of us, would do our cause more harm than good.

While I am noticed here, Bradyn is completely unknown and Gille can pass mostly undetected. Their goal is to listen and learn.

"She is approaching," Bradyn says excitedly from his position by the tent flap.

I move to leave when Gille stops me with a hand on my arm.

"You are not doing this for Moray's support alone."

I freeze.

"I have known you for more than seven years, Erik, and not once have I seen you this way." His gaze holds mine. "Not even with Isolda."

At the mention of her name, I close my eyes.

"It was not your fault, Erik."

Aye, it was very much so, but we will not argue the point again, especially not now. Opening my eyes, I move toward the entrance.

"I didn't bring up Isolda to upset you," Gille says quietly, "only to prove a point. This is not the same. *You* are not the same."

Of course he is right.

I turn.

"Aye, she is . . . different."

Gille does not seem surprised by my admission.

Other than sending Bradyn over with the invitation, I avoided talk of Reyne all day long, all the while fretting that she was done with me, that she'd not speak to me again. Only after my squire returned with the news she would indeed join me this eve did I tell Gille of my admission to her. But he said little about it, until now.

"I know her from her childhood," I say, something Gille already knows. "She has grown into a woman, more beautiful than I could have imagined. And the spark of her youth is still there at times . . ." I stop, realizing he does not fully understand.

"She lost her sister in a drowning, an incident she herself witnessed," I say in explanation.

Bradyn pops his head back in through the flap. "She is here," he says, his face beaming.

I move to follow him, but Gille catches me by the arm.

"Do this for yourself. Not for Cettina. Not for Edingham. They've both taken more of you than any man I know."

I hold his gaze, understanding, although I'm unsure whether I'm capable of doing as he bids.

"Come outside with me," I say instead.

And when I open the flap of the tent, I know Gille is right.

Though more simply dressed than last night, Reyne is no less elegant. She stands before us, chin held high, Warin on her arm.

Does he know what transpired?

"Good eve, Reyne. Warin. I expect you remember Sir Gille Elliot, and my squire, Bradyn."

They file out of the tent, moving to one side of Reyne and her brother. She bows not to me but to Bradyn. "Sir Bradyn, if it pleases you."

Her deference to him, which completely ignores their relative ranks, makes my squire inordinately happy. He beams and my heart warms toward her even more.

"He will earn his spurs before long," I agree. "Will you join us, Warin?"

Although I hope he will say nay, it would be considered highly offensive if I refrained from asking.

"I leave that decision to my sister."

Reyne gives him a look, and I know she has not told him she's learned of the arrangement.

"Lord Stokerton was a gentleman last eve, and I would expect no less at supper."

I would not be so sure of that, but I say not a word.

"Very well. Then I leave my sister to your care."

Every single one of us present, save Bradyn, understands the unusual nature of such an arrangement.

"I will escort her back safely, as I did last eve."

It was an easy feat given Reyne was not speaking with me by the time I left her at the tents.

"Any word?" he asks, and I know what he refers to, of course.

"Nay. But Gille will inform you of our strategy, if it pleases you."

I offer my arm. "Reyne?"

She hesitates a moment before taking it.

I lift the flap and escort her inside.

"A modest supper, if it pleases you."

"Oh!" Reyne exclaims as the candlelit table comes into view. "I should have expected as much. You are a Curia commander, of course."

If she had come into the tent earlier this day, Reyne might have had a very different reaction. I will have to thank Gille and Bradyn, again, for their assistance.

When I pull the modest chair out for her to sit, and she does, I move to my own as I fill both our goblets, with her permission.

"I did not think you would come," I admit.

"I wasn't sure I should."

I've dined with kings and queens. With nobles so influential they could have changed the course of my life if they'd chosen to do so.

But somehow this supper, this impromptu affair, feels like the most important of my life. Because something tells me this night will determine everything.

"Whether 'tis a good decision or nay, I am glad you are here." I raise my goblet. "To you, Lady Reyne, and your first adventure beyond the walls of Blackwell Castle."

She lifts her goblet cautiously.

We drink, and when Bradyn brings the meat he and Gille cooked themselves, we eat our repast. As the tent grows darker, our conversation deepens beyond politesse. As we finish the spiced pears Bradyn purchased at today's market, Reyne gives me a probing look and says, "I did not see you today."

"We did not venture far. Rawlins's threat has altered my purpose here."

I'm honest with Reyne, telling her all of what I've learned . . . which doesn't go far beyond what she and Warin already discovered. It is unusual for me to be so open—Gille often complains that I am too reticent with information—yet I find I want to share myself with her.

But as we finish eating, the conversation turns from Rawlins's plot to last eve's revelations. I apologize once again.

"I'd have told you about Isolda earlier."

"Will you do so now?"

Although plenty of people have gossiped about the would-be match, I rarely speak of it. But I will break my silence for Reyne—she deserves to hear the story.

"As I've said, she was a lady in waiting to Cettina. She is the daughter of a minor Borderland lord. For a time, I thought myself in love with her."

"Were you not?"

A question easily answered.

"Nay. Though we got on well enough." I'm unsure how to explain. "My father was pleased when King Malcom brought me to the capital, but he was also concerned for our family. As you know, I have no brother or sister to inherit the lands.

I promised that I would one day return, when needed, and Isolda, even though a Borderer, seemed a good match."

Reyne listed intently, perhaps too much so. But now that I'd started, there is no choice but to finish.

"She was a beautiful woman. Desired by many men at court, including Lord Bowes."

Reyne clearly knows who he is by her reaction. Of course, who in Edingham does not? It's not every day a king executes a noble for carrying on with his daughter.

"One eve, so late at night I'd been sleeping, Isolda came to my bedchamber, crying. She confessed that she and Lord Bowes had been"—I clear my throat—"intimate."

Reyne reaches for her goblet, a good thing, as the tale has only just begun.

"She confessed that she'd been seduced by him . . . and found a letter addressed to Lady Hilla in his chamber."

I can see she understands where this story leads. Anyone on the Isle would have been able to finish it for me.

"Isolda told me that she'd been upset I refused to profess my love to her, despite that we were getting married. Lord Bowes had seduced her, said he loved her. That night, the second time they had been together according to Isolda, she spied a letter in his chamber addressed to the princess. In it, he said he thoroughly enjoyed their time together and, despite that Lady Hilla was married, he would never stop fighting for them to be together."

I forge ahead, despite the tightening in my chest as I recall the events of that night.

"I was angry, of course. At Isolda for her unfaithfulness. But more so at Lord Bowes for his actions, seducing a woman betrothed and another married, and the princess no less. Rather than think through the repercussions, I turned, in anger, to the king. Told him what I'd learned and demanded Lord Bowes's chamber be searched. The letter was indeed found, and seemed to confirm what had long been whispered— Lady Hilla and Lord Bowes were having an affair." I shrug. "I assume you know the rest."

King Malcom *did* punish Bowes, by beheading him. And he exiled both Lady Hilla and her husband.

"What happened to Lady Isolda?"

"She fled to Stoughrock. I've not spoken to her since that night. And, as you know, though I never mentioned Lady Hilla to anyone other than the king, Bowes publicly named her as his mistress before he died."

"Leading the king to banish her and name Cettina as queen."

"Aye."

I'm unsure precisely what I expected, sharing my role in a story that altered the future of our kingdom. But when Reyne pushes back her chair and makes to leave, I do not blame her.

REYNE

I have been unsure for so long.

Of my purpose. Of how I would live without Fara. Of coming here, to this tourney. And now of Erik and how I should proceed with him.

But as he speaks of his part in the Hilla affair, I am finally sure of something.

Erik is in great pain, and my need to comfort him is stronger than any other consideration. It is a silly fancy, of course. This warrior does not need my pity—he is the queen's commander, a powerful and respected man—and yet, I can see the pain in his eyes.

He stands, and I realize he thinks I mean to leave.

I lay my hand on his arm, stopping him.

"I will give you nine days." I pause, then add, "You are not to blame for what happened, Erik."

He defies my words with a look that says otherwise.

"I should never have gone to Malcom."

"I should never have asked my sister if she wanted to dip her feet in the water with me."

My hand drops. Only my brother and parents know the details of my own painful story.

"We'd done so before, but that day . . . the river raged. 'Twas so hot, and so I made the suggestion that saw my sister killed. I am the reason she is gone." The familiar swell of tears threatens, but I push it away. "She leaned forward for the briefest of moments, and that was all it took. She fell in. When I saw her in the water . . ."

It is as if I'm sitting on that riverbank even now. I can smell the dirt and grass behind me, feel the breeze off the water. See Fara as she is swept away.

I close my eyes, trying to make the vision stop. When Erik's arms wrap around me, I cling to him as I did my brother when he pulled me from that very water.

"I jumped in and nearly drowned," I say against his shoulder. "So many times I've wished I had."

Oddly, I do not cry, as if I have no tears left inside me. Even so, being engulfed in Erik's arms offers a measure of comfort I never knew I needed.

"If I told you again 'twas not your fault your sister was killed, would you believe me?" he says, moving my hair to one side.

"Nay," I whisper.

"Is there anything I can say that would comfort you?"

I think on that for a moment. "Nay, I do not believe there is."

He pulls back, but I remain in his arms. "Then I will not try."

And without warning, his head lowers toward mine. Erik's lips touch my own, so gently at first I can hardly feel it. Though it *is* pleasant.

He pulls away and looks at me.

I blink.

"That was quite nice." Still, I'm disappointed it wasn't

more like the kisses I've read about in books. My world hasn't shaken, nor do my knees feel weak.

"Nice. Have you not been kissed before, Reyne?"

I raise my chin. "Aye, I have."

And then I admit, "That was my second."

"And your first kiss, was it like that one?"

"Aye. 'Twas pleasant enough."

He has the same look as Warin did when he escorted me here. As if he knows something I do not. Except I know my brother's secret and I do not know what Erik hides from me. His smile is as amused as it is suddenly playful.

"Pleasant. Nice."

"Aye."

"Hmmm."

I have no time to interpret the sound before he lowers his head again. When his lips meet mine this time, his tongue is there as well, gliding along the folds of my mouth.

"Open for me, Reyne."

I am unsure what he means. Fara's books spoke of passion and desire, and even of kissing, but they make no mention of how it is done.

I open my mouth to ask Erik for further instruction, but before I am able, his tongue glides inside and touches my own. At first the shock eclipses all other feelings, but then I start to wonder what, precisely, I should do. Fortunately, there is no need. Erik shows me.

And when I touch my tongue fully to his, he groans.

His mouth completely covers mine as he tilts his head to the side. Taking his lead, I kiss him back, until much later, breathless, Erik pulls away. I stare at his mouth and lips in wonder. So the books weren't stuff and nonsense after all. How could he have aroused such feelings in me this quickly?

"Your tongue," I say, only then realizing how ridiculous that sounds. "I did not know."

"That, my dear Reyne, was your first kiss. The other was nothing more than a touching of our lips. A greeting."

I laugh. "I have greeted many people before, Erik, and can assure you, I do not do so with my lips."

He is so handsome when he smiles.

"A proper kiss cannot be described with words such as nice. Or pleasant. A proper kiss makes you crave more."

"If that is so, then aye, that was my first kiss." Because I most certainly *do* crave more.

For a moment I think he will kiss me again. Instead, Erik releases me and runs his hand through his hair.

"If we stay here, I will show you what else my tongue can do, dear Reyne. And that will not do."

In fact, I think it would do nicely. But I don't say so aloud, because he still has not answered my question. Does he love another?

Unwilling to ruin this moment, I choose not to ask again. But I will, soon.

Mayhap after I learn what else, precisely, he can do with his tongue.

ERIK

"*Y*ou can taste the bitterness, on the tip of your tongue," I say to the men sitting around the fire. Each night Gille, Bradyn, and I have come here to the Moray tents. Reyne and I continue to dance around our mutual desire, our eyes meeting more than once.

Mentioning my tongue in conversation has become a private jest between us these past three days. And although my attention should be fixed on Lord Rawlins and the threat he poses, I find this seduction of Reyne has captured too much of it.

"Do they teach ya at the capital how to taste ale?" a man named John asks.

I resist looking toward Reyne, whose father and brother are sitting with us, after all. Instead, I answer his question with a smile. Meant for her.

"Nay," I say, "I've learned on my own."

I do look at her then.

"Ale is a special interest of mine."

She gives me a look as if to say, *stop*. Which I most certainly will not.

"If brewed correctly, there is no better taste than . . . ale."

Enjoying jesting with her, I continue until she leaps up and walks away. Without reacting, I turn to Warin as the others continue discussing the merits of good ale.

"Have you discovered anything?"

Warin nods, standing. I follow him away from the fires as Gille walks up behind us.

"My father was in the stands for the saber toss, and he managed to position himself close to Rawlins."

Gille and I exchange a look.

"Did he say anything of import?"

Warin frowns. "Perhaps. Do you know an Elderman by the name of Father Aiken?"

I think back to the last time the Prima visited Breywood. The church's leader was accompanied by a contingent of guards.

"Aye," I say, remembering. "He was with Father Silvester at the queen's coronation, I believe."

"He was the one who never spoke," Gille adds. "Do you remember we discussed the possibility of him being one of Silvester's Shadow Warriors?"

I can envision him standing at the side of the hall now. Never eating. Never speaking. And though Silvester has never identified his secret army or acknowledged that they in fact exist, all know of them. Throughout the years these highly skilled fighters, who take the same vows as the Eldermen, have made targeted attacks to help advance the Prima's agenda. Some of the time, they enforce the church's laws. Once, a minor border lord thought to encroach on land owned by the church, reasoning the only building on it, an old monastery, had not been used in years. But the Shadow Warriors either chased away or killed every man within its boundaries. There are other occasions when their might is used for reasons of political expediency.

"What of this Father Aiken?" I ask. "And what is his connection to Rawlins's meeting?"

"Maybe none," Warin admits. "But Rawlins mentioned him by name, which leads me to believe he may be here. Have you seen any of the Prima's men at this tourney?"

Gille frowns. "The church's warriors do not participate in tournaments."

Increasingly, over the years, the church has distanced itself from such things. Father Silvester would preach about "excess" and "immodesty." And though most on the Isle are believers, with the exception of the Voyagers of Murwood End, even the most loyal among them have begun to question the Prima's increasingly stringent interpretation of the church's teachings.

"Precisely," Warin agrees. "So why is he here, if indeed it is true?"

We fall silent.

Why indeed?

He has not shown himself. Though hundreds attend this event, a hooded man would have been easy to spot, presuming he was not dressed in disguise. And if he had been in attendance, surely others would likely have remarked on it.

"You believe the church is involved in whatever Rawlins has planned?" I ask the obvious question.

"I think it possible," Warin says.

"We need to be at that meeting," Gille says.

"What will we do," Warin asks, "if we discover its whereabouts? Surely we cannot simply stroll in and ask for seats?"

"Surely not," I agree. "But we've limited choices to make unless we at least learn where it is being held." I clasp Warin's shoulder. "Gille and I are glad to have an ally in this, at least."

Warin gives me a look, and though we've not discussed

Reyne, who asked me not to reveal that I shared the truth with her, something passes between us.

An understanding. An alliance, of sorts.

"If I were my father, I'd speak to the men," he says. "War with Meria will help no one."

"Nay, it will not." I remove my hand. "Tell it to the nobles who believe 'twould be best to strike while Galfrid is weak."

Warin smiles. "'Tis your job, is it not?"

Gille laughs. "Precisely why we are here. At least, precisely why *I* am here. I begin to wonder about this one."

My friend nudges my arm as both of my companions laugh, and I find myself glancing back at the fire to see if Reyne has returned.

"Do you see?" Gille shakes his head. "Your sister has captivated him."

She has indeed.

*H*ow is it possible that just one day remains?

In some ways, this has been the most pleasurable time of my life. Attending feasts and celebrations, cheering for Erik and my brother. Strolling through the market yesterday with my father, something I'd never done before in my life.

As predicted, I've enjoyed pretending not to know of his design. I've made quite a show of feigning surprise whenever he allows me to be escorted by Erik, unattended. And though I should not revel in others' discomfort, I remind myself that had Erik not told me at Havefest, I would be the only Moray here not privy to the queen's commander's true purpose here.

Although we've been alone twice since that kiss, we've not repeated it. Though I am not aware of Erik's reasons for holding back, my own are simple.

I am falling for him, and if I kiss him again, my fate will be decided, or as good as. So I pine for him instead . . . and remain undecided. Erik is all that I knew him to be. Suited to me in every way save one.

I still haven't repeated my question about the queen.

Tomorrow is the last day of the tourney, however, and I cannot delay any further. I will ask him again this very eve at the feast. If he refuses to answer, I will take it as an affirmative, and return home without the promise of marriage.

"You are quiet, sister," Warin says as we move into the great hall.

"I've much to think on," I admit. "As do you."

After days of attempting to learn the location of this secret meeting, Gille finally believes he's done so. When he spotted Rawlins among the tents, he followed him to the dovecote hidden in the woods on the edge of Ledenhill's land.

Though he remained there for more than two hours and saw no one else enter or exit, they have not found a better lead. Erik, Gille, and Warin all plan to sleep among the trees this eve, out of sight of the dovecote but close enough to see if, indeed, this was the location of the secret meeting.

In some ways it feels as if I have already agreed to the match. Erik and my brother grow closer each day, and Father seems to have welcomed the son of his former friend into our camp and, perhaps, our lives.

And I want to . . . more than I've let myself want anything for a long time. But first I must know.

"You look beautiful this eve."

I did not see Erik coming, but the voice from behind me is easily recognizable.

"Good eve, Erik," I say, Warin, my father and his men moving ahead.

Turning, I nearly gasp. "You look so . . . official."

His surcoat is not one I've seen on him before, not even at Havefest. It is emblazoned with the Tree of Loigh, the silver lining so bright it resembles real silver, which it very well may be. He has shaved, the beginnings of a beard now gone, Erik's defined cheekbones on full display.

He looks less like the queen's commander than he does a king.

"You do not approve?"

In fact, he is as handsome as ever, but my thoughts remind me of why this union may not be. Feelings rage within me, a strange mix I cannot control, and I know I cannot wait until the evening is over to speak to him. The feast will not begin for hours.

"I approve," I say cautiously. "But I would speak to you. Alone."

His eyes bore into mine. "Your tone is troubling," he says.

Something has been troubling *me* for nigh a sennight, and he's standing just before me. "Do you think there is a place we might speak?"

Erik is not the only one dressed in his finest. I've saved this gown for this eve's celebration, and from the way Erik is eyeing the low neckline, he approves.

I clear my throat.

"Apologies," he says, turning. "Though not really," I think I hear him mumble.

Smiling, I follow him from the hall and down the stairs, realizing we are headed back into the courtyard.

"Where are we going?"

Just as I ask, Erik offers his arm, and I realize I know precisely where he is bringing me. Indeed, in no time, after leaving the main keep, we pass the small courtyard where Havefest was held and walk up the cobblestone path.

"No cushions this eve," he says as we reach the alcove. "But ample light . . ." He tilts his head up, as do I, to see the torch just above us. ". . . so that I may enjoy the beautiful sight before me."

Licking my lips, which have suddenly gone dry, I sit and

attempt to avoid gawking at him. Sitting across from me, he leans over and takes my hands.

"What is wrong, Reyne?"

How can he not already know?

"Tomorrow is the last day," I say. "And then you will leave for the capital, and I for home."

He does not react. "And that is how you would have it? That we part on the morrow?"

Just like that other night in this very same spot, I wish that he would kiss me. That we could avoid this discussion that might tear us apart forever. There is so much more to explore with him, the passion he promised just within reach.

Father approves.

Warin approves.

Mother would gladly take Erik Stokerton as a son-in-law.

"I do not know," I say honestly. "All want this match but . . ."

"But you?"

He looks angry. And maybe that is a good thing. He clearly wishes to marry me. But is it only for my father's support? How can he not understand the reason matters? And more importantly, *she* matters.

"I asked you once if you loved the queen, and you did not answer me. Yet you wish for us to announce our betrothal tomorrow. So I ask you again, do you love her?"

His expression reveals nothing. "Marry."

I clasp my hands together and squeeze. "Pardon?"

"I wish for us to marry, not become betrothed. Your father made it clear I'd not have his support until we were married."

My jaw drops.

"Here? At Ledenhill? Without my mother present? With no gown or feast or . . . marry here?" I repeat.

Erik frowns. "I know it is not the wedding ceremony you

would have. Nor is it the one you deserve. But vows to join as man and wife, with proper witnesses, are all that is necessary. As you know."

Wed. Tomorrow?

"Even if we learn nothing from the dovecote, I must get back to the capital. Cettina needs to know about it."

Cettina. It serves as a reminder, not that I needed it, that he has not yet answered me.

"I can do without a grand ceremony," I respond. "Or even my mother as witness, if such is necessary. But I cannot do without an answer to the question I've asked twice now. Do you love her?"

Erik's jaw clenches. He opens his mouth, and then closes it again.

I know the answer before he gives it.

"Aye."

18

ERIK

I should have given a more nuanced answer, but I refuse to lie to Reyne again.

"I did not answer you before because the answer is not so simple as it seems."

I've hurt her and am sorry for it.

"It is not difficult to be captivated by Cettina," I begin, knowing this does not help my cause. "As her personal guard, I got to know her well. I knew from the start she was different from King Malcom. Though her mother died before I came to court, most say Cettina is very much like her."

I hate the pain in Reyne's eyes, so I rush to finish my story.

"It was only after the affair, when Isolda left Breywood, when I was at my lowest, that I came to understand what a remarkable woman she is. Cettina stood up to her father in front of the Curia, even though she was not then allowed to attend those meetings. She barged into the room and demanded her sister be allowed to present her case to the group before the sentence was carried out. And when her father refused, Cettina began to appeal one by one to the Curia on her own, risking her father's wrath."

Reyne's only reaction is to wring her hands on her lap.

"After Lord Bowes was beheaded, and Lady Hilla and Lord Whitley, her husband, were banished from court, Cettina began to campaign almost immediately for their return. When her father became sick, and she was thrust into the role of queen, she appointed me as second commander. And she has been fighting for Edingham ever since." I pause, taking in the way Reyne sits there, so still and stiff. "Do I love her? A woman who elevated a man whom she could have banished from court for his role in the affair? Who refuses to allow even the most powerful men in the kingdom to sway her beliefs? I do, Reyne. But not in the way you think."

I wait for her to respond.

"So you love her . . . as you would a sister?" she says haltingly.

I should say aye, but I want her to make this decision knowing all. "I've not had a sister, so I do not know how to answer that."

"As a friend, then?"

I shrug helplessly. Again, it is hard to answer the question. Cettina is so different from any other friend I've had.

"Have you kissed her?"

"Aye."

"It was but once, and we knew immediately 'twas a mistake. It was the night after the coronation, which she never expected to happen. That crown weighs as heavy on her head now as it did that eve, but she is learning to bear it."

"You have not made love to her?"

"Nay."

"But you do love her."

I cannot do this any longer . . . not without touching her.

So I lower onto the small stone seat beside her and take her hands in mine.

"The rumors are understandable," I say. "She is a beautiful woman." Reyne tries to pull her hands away, but I squeeze them tighter instead. "And a young woman. I am the only member of the Curia within ten years of her age. And perhaps there was a spark of something once, but that was born of loneliness and grief. It was not this . . . it was nothing like what is between us."

Her laugh is a bitter one. "You mean a spark born out of a possible alliance?"

I refuse to let her leave here thinking that is all that exists between us. "There is more here, and well you know it, Reyne."

She doesn't respond.

"I am not in love with Cettina as you imagine it. Love takes many forms, does it not? You've read the Garra's teachings. Love of your siblings. Your parents. Love, for you, of reading and writing. And for me, of training boys like Bradyn. I did not answer your question the first time you asked it, Reyne, because I wanted us to get the chance to know each other as we are now. Now, the choice is yours."

If there's any hope she will give any indication of her answer, that hope is dashed when she stands, pulling me up with her.

"We will be missed."

I cannot let her leave like this.

"Reyne." I cup her beautiful face. "Know this. Your father offered your hand to me, but only you can truly give it. I know many men who falsely believe they know better than a woman simply because they've a prick in their pants, but I can assure you I'm not one of them."

Finally, a smile.

"I have told you from the start what we plan here. And if

you do consent to marry me, you will never be treated as if your opinion is unimportant or inconsequential. You won't just be my seat partner at meals or the manager of the castle staff after we return to the Highlands. You will be my wife in all things, and you will have my devotion, always."

But she wants more. I can see it in her eyes.

Reyne wants my love as well.

I adore her. Desire her. Want to feel her underneath me as I claim her body. I want to be the man to bring the light back into her eyes.

But I cannot say I love her. Not yet. We need more than a sennight to know each other, but Reyne and I are out of time.

"There!" Warin whispers. "Do you see it?"

We are hidden in the trees so well that it is difficult to discern much at all. I see the dovecote but nothing else.

"Nay," I whisper back. "Where?"

But no sooner have the words left my lips than I notice it. A barely perceptible movement, and then two men emerge.

"MacKinnish," Gille says. "Not a surprise at all."

Nay, though it *is* a surprise that we guessed correctly about the location. Were these men truly responsible for the attack on Saitford Village? And for planning another similar attack?

Gille moves, but I hold him back.

"Nay, we wait until all arrive."

We've little choice but to arrest these men, and it's been agreed we will do so on my authority as the queen's commander. But first, I'd learn how many others are involved.

"There he is," Gille says.

Rawlins. And two men with him. My hand itches as it

rests upon my sword hilt. I crane my neck upward as a bird calls out above us, as if to give away our location. But none of the men now entering the dovecote even glance our way. They've no suspicion they might be watched. At least that is to our advantage.

A few moments later, MacKinnish emerges, as if waiting for someone. He looks in every direction, including ours, but doesn't find what he seeks.

Who is he waiting for?

I listen to Warin and Gille breathing. I listen to the leaves rustling in the trees above us, the quiet, as always, more disconcerting than sounds of battle. With swords clanging and horses neighing, there is no doubt about what lies ahead.

Blood. Death. Families torn apart.

But here, in this silent field as we witness the worst sort of treachery, the hairs rise on the back of my neck. I turn, sensing something is amiss. Warin and Gille seem on alert too, but nothing moves around us.

Thankfully, we look back just in time to see him. Another man, walking alone, from a different direction than the others. I squint, knowing he is familiar to me but not recognizing him until his face fully comes into view.

The queen's brother-in-law.

"Goddammit."

Warin doesn't react, but Gille does, and strongly too.

"That bastard. I will send him to hell myself."

If anyone were to send him to hell, it would be me. Though no one truly knows the details of what happened between us, I stand, prepared to do just that, when someone behind us growls out, "Do not move."

How did he get so close without making a sound?

"Father Aiken," Gille correctly says. "We'd heard you might be here."

The Elderman's hood covers the top portion of his face. His sword at the ready, Father Aiken prepares to fight.

So he *is* a Shadow Warrior? For no mortal man could sneak up on us that way.

Of course, I know the stories are not true. Gille and I have speculated the Prima is responsible for the rumors, that he perhaps spread them to gain more power. This man is mortal, as are the other Shadow Warriors, even though this is the first time I've come face-to-face with one who is known to me.

I defy him and unsheathe my sword.

"You are outnumbered," I say, offering a silent prayer that I am speaking the truth. There are several men in the dovecote, aye, but we are a distance away.

Without removing his hood, he says, "If I wanted you dead, all three of you would be so already."

His voice is low but piercing.

"You do not want to go down there," he says. I can only assume he speaks of the dovecote.

"Nay?" Warin taunts back. "Instead, you'd have your friends butcher more innocent women and children?"

He does not flinch. "They are not my friends. Put down your swords, and I will do the same."

Gille laughs. "I think not, Elderman."

I was little more than a boy when I faced thousands of enemy soldiers at the Battle of Hendrelds. But now, standing across from this lone man, I am more afraid than I've ever been in my life. He did have the advantage, and lost it by revealing himself. Even so, the Shadow Warrior has the look of a man who is confident he will win if we force a fight on him. And, illogical as it seems, I believe him . . . such a fight would probably leave him mortally wounded, but that would be little comfort to three dead men.

Fighting Father Aiken is not something I wish to do this day. Not until I learn what he came here to tell us.

"Do it," I command.

Both Gille and Warin hesitate.

"That was not a request."

I've no desire to pull rank on either of them, most especially Warin, who barely recognizes me as his superior. But neither will I get them killed this day.

"Now," I repeat.

When they sheathe their swords, I do the same. Only then does Aiken set down his own weapon. We may no longer be armed, but the mood is like death sitting at the very tip of a sword.

"I am expected at that meeting, and plan to attend," Aiken says.

We should not have lowered our weapons.

"We will meet here after the melee," he continues, "and I will tell you of what they plan."

Another bitter laugh, this time from Warin. "So you can return with those bastards to kill us all for discovering your treachery?"

"Why would we do such a thing?" I ask, studying him.

The Elderman lowers his hood.

One word comes to mind: deadly. His eyes, most especially.

"If you do not, those who believe as these men do, and there are more of them, will carry out the very attack you are here to prevent. Arrest them with no proof of anything other than conducting a secret meeting, and you accomplish nothing. Would you have the blood of another Saitford on your hands?"

I can feel the anger oozing off both men beside me, but I keep my eyes on Aiken, looking for any sign of treachery. He is too skilled to reveal anything, however.

"Why are you here?" I ask.

His answer is immediate. "That"—he nods toward the dovecote—"is my mission."

"To discover the men who plan an attack on innocent people?" Warin guesses.

Aiken looks directly at me. "To help them carry out that attack."

Gille gasps. "You . . ."

For the first time since he appeared, I relax my stance, defeated. Aiken represents the Prima, which means the church is indeed involved. They are supporting Lord Hinton as the heir to King Galfrid, and now they are trying to goad us into battle with Meria. Why?

"They knew Saitford would happen?" I ask.

"We helped," he says calmly, as if not wishing to admit he took part in a massacre against innocents.

"We? The church?"

"The Prima," he clarifies.

It is an important distinction. Although the Prima is the head of the church and the one person who should perpetuate its teachings, Father Silvester's extreme views have alienated some.

Maybe even within their own ranks?

"You are the devil," Gille spits, and I do not disagree.

Aiken keeps his gaze on me. "Will you deal with the devil, then? You must decide, and quickly."

I could ask why he does this, why he so obviously goes against the orders of the man he serves, if Aiken's true purpose is to stop the next attack. But I have a feeling he won't freely reveal his motivations.

Our choice is a simple one. We march across the field in front of us, arrest the men within the dovecote, and take them back to the capital for punishment. One they will receive, for Cettina will certainly believe us.

But will anyone else? Those who oppose the queen could use this as a reason to condemn her . . . especially if she punishes these men and the attack happens anyway.

Our other choice? As Aiken so aptly put it, a deal with the devil. If we agree to treat with him, we may learn enough to prevent the slaughter from happening at all—and to completely hamstring those who would wish for another Saitford.

Or we may be cut down this very night by an ambush of men wishing to silence those who would expose them.

"I raise suspicions by being late," he says in that deadly calm, deadpan voice.

There is no good choice here, but one must be made.

"Go. We will return when the melee has ended."

Gille and Warin immediately begin to protest, but I put my hand up to silence them. I've made my decision and will not waver.

With luck, I will be alive long enough to learn Reyne's answer. And perhaps even long enough to know if the decision I just made was the correct one.

19

REYNE

I watch with horror as the two sides prepare to cut down, kidnap, and otherwise decimate the men across the field from them. My father, leader of Team Azure, is positioned at the edge of the field with a Highland lord I do not recognize, who, judging by his green surcoat, is marshal and leader of Team Vert. Their mounts dance under them.

I can easily spot Erik among them, riding side by side with my brother. I assume the man riding the black destrier on Erik's other side is Gille. The crowd around me is cheering wildly, but by the time the horn sounds, I am torn between closing my eyes and running down to the field for a better view.

As the men charge toward one another, I squeeze my eyes shut.

"'Tis a horrific sight, is it not?"

When I open them again, the woman next to me points to the painted white lines now visible on the field.

"If they are able to push men from the opposing side across that line, they are well and truly captured."

The woman smiles. She is not much older than me, dressed in a simple but well-made kirtle. Her hair is loose, long, and brown, and her eyes are warm and bright. Like sunshine beams out from within her.

"Lady Arabelle," she says, "pleased to make your acquaintance."

"I am Lady Reyne, daughter of Lord Moray. And very pleased to make yours."

I've lost Erik and my brother in the chaos. Some of the men have already lost their mounts in the melee. Squires lead horses to the side of the field as the echoes of swordplay reach us, even from this far away.

"'Tis brutal," I say.

"Meant to prepare them for real battle. Aye."

Warin explained the modifications to their weapons. The lances are all blunted, making the fight as safe as possible, but it looks very real from this vantage point.

"Do you cheer for Vert or Azure?" I ask Lady Arabelle.

"Vert," she says, "though I mostly cheer for my husband not to be injured. Did you know a man died three years ago at this tourney?"

"Aye," I say, wincing as one rider's horse topples with him on it.

"In that very way," she says, "crushed by the weight of his horse."

Thankfully, it seems that sad incident will not be repeated this day. Or at least not yet. Both horse and rider are righted but also captured and brought across the white line to Azure.

"So you are from the North?" I ask.

The two sides that fight in the melee are almost always split by region, and this year it is north versus south. Our castle sits closer to the capital, but not so far south we could ever be mistaken as anything other than Highlanders. My homeland, surrounded by mountains on every side, is as wild as it is beautiful.

"Aye," she says, "though I am not a Highlander born. I was raised just south of Galmouth Bay."

My attention is torn from the field.

"Where Meria was to attack?"

She nods. "Aye."

If the Oryan had not sunk, they say it would have landed in Galmouth Bay, its soldiers heading northwest to the border from there.

I shudder, wondering so many things as we watch the false battle play out before us, men kidnapping and injuring each other in a much tamer version of what could very well unfold if Erik is unsuccessful in averting war.

I cannot watch any longer.

Instead, I stare across the field to the treetops beyond it. I don't know what transpired this morn. Erik and my brother slept among the trees last eve, and the first time I saw them today was on the field.

Did they discover anything at the dovecote?

And what, precisely, am I to do this day?

Erik's answer last eve left me with more questions. I wish for more time, but I know we've run out.

A loud cheer forces my attention back onto the field. Soon no lances remain on the field, and as more and more men are "kidnapped," the remainder are left unseated and on their feet. I find some measure of peace in knowing neither Warin nor Erik will be trampled or crushed to death.

"There is my husband," Lady Arabelle cries. She points to a man wearing the green emblazoned surcoat. "Oh dear," she says just as two men in blue capture him, one on each side.

Her shoulders sag. "He can little afford the price he'll pay for that."

"What do you mean?"

I know some of the rules of the melee but not all.

"Is it not just one silver coin to be released?"

She shakes her head. "Aye, but look more closely. Both he and his weapon must be ransomed, and a different man picked up his sword."

Looking more closely, I realize that although Lady Arabelle's kirtle is well-made, it is simply adorned.

"Does it not cost more to ransom a man than his sword?"

My companion shakes her head.

"Not a sword forged in Murwood End. It was given to him by his grandfather. I told him not to bring it here, but my husband is stubborn."

I look more closely and realize the man now armed with two swords is none but Erik. I scream as he is ambushed from behind. He fights his opponent off as poor Lady Arabelle's husband is dragged down the lengthy field.

The attacker retreats, and Erik appears safe, for now.

"Is that your husband?"

"Nay." I watch as Bradyn runs onto the field in full armor and takes the sword from Erik.

"Your relative?"

I search the field for Warin but do not see him.

"He is either a man I knew in my childhood," I say as the crowd cheers, though I cannot discern the reason, "or he will be my husband."

Lady Arabelle's eyes widen.

"Truly?"

There is no simple way to explain.

"He and my father wish to forge an alliance with our marriage. The decision, it seems, has been left to me."

If she was surprised by my announcement of a possible marriage, she is much more so at this bit of news.

"I've never heard of such a thing before."

She speaks in earnest, her words a needed reminder that

despite this week's deception my father has treated me kindly since Fara's passing. And yet . . .

"Should we not all be given such a choice? In *Pedair Cainc y Hempswood*, the author, a Garra and direct descendant of Athea, says that even married women should be allowed to make and sign agreements and bear witness in disputes."

Lady Arabelle does not seem to agree. "I know nothing of *Pedair Cainc y Hempswood*, but my father says the teachings of the Garra are dangerous. Even my mother forbids mention of them."

Dangerous indeed. Though not for women, surely.

"If given the choice, I do believe I would have married my husband," she continues. "He is not wealthy but treats me kindly. Is your knight not kind?"

I look for Erik.

"He is very much so."

"Old, then?"

I scan the field but can make out nothing beyond a tangle of men and bodies and swords.

"Nay. He is young, and quite comely."

"Ah, so he is poor?"

Sighing, I spot him. Safe, for now.

"Nay. He is the queen's second commander," I tell her, watching her expression.

Lady Arabelle's jaw drops. "You are to marry Lord Stokerton?"

I wait for her to understand.

"But he is," her voice trails off.

"Precisely."

"Oh."

Is there anyone who has not heard of Cettina and Erik? None know he was betrothed to one of her ladies. Or of his role in the Hilla affair. But all seem to be aware of the rumors about him and the queen.

"I do not wish to marry a man who loves another."

Lady Arabelle spins toward me suddenly, taking me by surprise.

"I know you not at all, so please, I beg you to forgive my forwardness. I am unable to read or write, and have traveled little, save from my old home to the new one. But I fancied myself in love with a young man once. The son of the village butcher. But now I do very much love my husband."

She blinks rapidly, as if awaiting my response. It strikes me that I miss this—having another woman to confide in. I lost that when Fara died. She was my sister, aye, but also my best friend.

"Even if he loves her," she whispers, "that does not mean he cannot love you more. She may be the Queen of Edingham"—Lady Arabelle smiles—"but you would be his wife."

Another cheer pulls our attention to the field. Many men were eliminated during our talk, it seems.

"Is that not him?" she asks, pointing to Erik as he stands over an opponent, his sword tip to the man's chest.

"Aye," I say, watching, holding my breath until he pulls back the sword. The man gets up and runs off toward our line. Lady Arabelle and I say nothing more as the few remaining combatants fight on foot. I cannot say part of me isn't relieved when Warin is "taken," for at least I know he is safe. And it is clear Azure has won, with at least twice as many men remaining as the other side. But there is an individual champion as well, the last man remaining on the field. The champion of the tourney, an honor Erik has claimed before.

And it is clear he intends to do so again this day. Only two men remain on the field, Erik being one of them.

"They say King Malcom himself brought Lord Stokerton to the capital after seeing him fight," Lady Arabelle says. "I don't recall seeing him here these past few years, but I suppose 'tis well enough he's let others be crowned champion. I do believe he would have won each year."

As he does now, Erik's opponent's sword flying from his hands as he deals the final blow. With shouts and cheers from both the stands and those watching from the sides of the field, the melee is declared at an end. My father, acting as marshal, takes off Erik's helmet and raises his hand into the air.

"He's looking this way!" Lady Arabelle exclaims.

Indeed, even from this distance, I can see his head swivel toward us. Does he know I am in these stands. Is he looking for me?

"He comes this way," Arabelle shrieks. "Do you see? He is coming here."

I see, quite clearly.

Amidst the cheers of the crowd around us, Erik leaves the field and, with each stride toward me, marks his intentions clearly.

My heart begins to slam inside my chest as I look at Arabelle.

"He is not marrying the queen," she says. "Go."

Could I possibly compete with a queen? Do I wish to try?

I stand and raise my skirts, feeling so many eyes on me as I descend the wooden stands, hastened along by the advice of a friendly stranger. How I wish I had taken my maid with me to the tournament. Someone, anyone I could speak to about this. My father and Warin would care little for my only objection to Erik. They would say I am being silly. But Fara would have understood my dilemma.

With my back to the stands, I wait. Finally, after what feels like days rather than minutes, Erik is before me. His face is streaked with dirt, the crest on his surcoat barely visible from the same. He says nothing but lays his sword on the ground at my feet, a distinctly Highland custom to show complete trust in another person. Then he kneels before me.

"I've captured ten men, two horses, and three swords this day. They are all yours, Lady Reyne, if you will have them."

The fighters on the winning side can choose to ransom those they've captured or return them for naught. They can apparently do the same with their property, some knights having made their fortunes this way. Others, like Arabelle's husband, have lost more than they can afford, although he will find mercy today.

Only one man, the tourney champion, can gift his earnings to another.

I alone know what he is asking. He offers me a wedding gift.

I look into his eyes as the crowd holds their collective breath behind me.

Accept the gift, accept him. Compete with a queen for his love.

Deny the gift, deny Erik, and return home to wonder what may have been.

This is my choice, and in my heart, I know I have already decided even as I pretend it is not so. I am a pawn, but the same is true of Erik in some ways.

"I accept your gift," I say, resolved. "And your hand in marriage."

ERIK

"*H*e's waiting for you."

Having just returned from our late-night meeting with the Elderman, I'm grateful to still have my head . . . yet there is still a chance I might lose it. I've not spoken to Moray since he learned Reyne has known about our agreement from the start. It is entirely possible he may withdraw his support.

Support the queen needs more than ever, given what we've just learned.

"Are you joining us?" I ask Warin.

He steps away from me and toward Gille.

"Nay," he says, "I think I will remain out here."

Traitor.

Instinctively, I look toward the tent where Reyne has stayed this past fortnight, even though I know she is no longer there, nor will she be coming back this eve.

With a final glance at the others, I lift the flap and enter the tent. Lord Moray is sitting at the table, wine goblet in hand, and he gestures to a seat across from him.

"Sit."

I am about to do so when he stops me.

"Pour yourself some wine first," he says gruffly.

Once seated, I wait for him to speak.

"A toast."

I can finally breathe again.

This is a betrothal agreement we are discussing. Not a secondary concern any longer, but one that drove me so hard this day. Cettina asked that I remind everyone why she chose me as commander. But I did not win for her today. I did so out of respect for this very man, and for his daughter.

"To a new alliance," he says, lifting his goblet.

"A new alliance," I agree.

Both of us drink, although he finishes first. "And if you ever lie to me again, I will serve your bollocks to the queen on a platter, commander or nay."

I nearly spit out my wine.

Thankfully, though Moray isn't exactly smiling, the twinkle in his eyes leads me to believe he is, possibly, jesting. Or not. It is hard to discern.

Either way, I refuse to make a promise I cannot keep.

"My allegiance will be to your daughter first, as it's been these past weeks. Barring that, I would never lie to you, Lord Moray."

I can't tell if the answer pleases him or angers him even more, but it matters not. It is the only answer I have.

"She deserved to know," I press, realizing I may well be making matters worse.

Moray's grunt indicates he clearly does not agree.

"Tell me of the Elderman," he says.

Moray already knew the details of that morning's meeting. But after Reyne agreed to become my wife—and then proceeded to give back every hard-earned prize I'd won that day, a gesture that pleased me more than she realized—we had little time to celebrate.

While Moray made arrangements for a small ceremony within Ledenhill's hall for the next day, all understanding the necessity of a quick return to the capital, I set off with Warin, Elliott, and six other Moray men.

Men who proved unnecessary.

"He was alone, just as he claimed he would be. He warned of another attack in one month's time."

"Do you believe him?"

"It matters not. Either way, we must send men to Firley Dinch. Either to stop an attack or defend against one. Neither of which will please the queen." Firley Dinch, the Merian border town, is one of the largest on either side of the Terese River.

Indeed, Cettina and the Curia will be enraged to learn that the attack on Saitford was no border dispute at all, but a concerted attempt to drag Edingham into a war with Meria, also engaged in by the Prima and several Highland lords.

And it is going to happen again.

"He could not have known, or planned for us to be in those woods this morn."

"How did he find you?"

There was only one answer that I could discern.

"I doubt not the man is a Shadow Warrior. Though why he works against the Prima now, I do not know. Mayhap the killing of innocents swayed him?"

Moray scowls. "If he is truly a Shadow Warrior, no death is more abhorrent than disobedience to the Prima."

I silently agree. They were trained to fight for and protect the Prima beyond all other duties. But I have no other explanation.

"Whatever his reasons for helping us, if that is his true intention, it matters not. If Rawlins and the others are exposed as traitors, I would expect the other Highlanders to stand down."

"They will do so. You have my word."

And now that he's given it, I must know.

"If your daughter had not agreed to marry me, what would you have done, knowing of this treachery from within? Would you have stood idly by and allowed Edingham to be drawn into a false war?"

Aside from Reyne, I've thought of little else. Moray chose once not to get involved, and our families' alliance paid the price. Would he have done the same again, even though innocents, albeit Merians, paid the ultimate price? Or would he have lent his support without this new alliance of ours?

Moray smiles, much as he did that first day.

"I suppose we will never know."

THIS IS NOT AT ALL what I expected my wedding ceremony to be. For a time, I imagined it would be held at court, Isolda by my side. Though I cannot say I loved her, she was a beautiful woman, and my father was pleased by the prospective alliance between our families. She cared for me too.

It had felt like enough.

After she fled, I trusted my instincts with women as little as my ability to make decisions devoid of emotion. I retreated into myself, doing my duties but attending no meals or feasts, training every spare moment. Still, I knew it could not last forever, that I would, one day, have to marry. The arrangement, I had thought, would be like my parents' wedding ceremony, made solely for the families' betterment.

I think of my parents, who should be here now. My mother will be disappointed, as will Reyne's, I am sure. My father will balk at first but be pleased by the outcome. He hates being at odds with a man he respects, whose lands border his own.

Some might say my wedding to Reyne is little different than theirs was all those years ago. The idea was not mine, but Moray's, and yet it feels different. I desire Reyne very much, but I also *like* her.

"She's coming."

Flanked by her father on one side, her brother on the other, Reyne appears at the hall's entrance, its inhabitants clearly happy to have capped their tournament celebrations with an impromptu wedding. The only one not so pleased is the Elderman, who has reluctantly agreed to marry us. He protested the lack of proper time between announcing the betrothal and this quick ceremony, arguing at least a sennight should pass between the two. His appeal for our exchange of vows to be held in front of Ledenhill's chapel had even been overruled, our host preferring to provide enough room for all wishing to attend the festivities.

I watch as Reyne approaches me through a sea of mostly strangers, pausing to kiss her father and then Warin, both of whom she has forgiven for their deceit. They peel away, leaving just the two of us. Or so it seems. Wearing the dress she donned the eve of Havefest, her hair falling around her shoulders in red waves of fire, Reyne looks at me.

In a few moments, this woman will be my wife. And although our wedding night may not be the one I'd like to give her, as we leave immediately after this ceremony for Breywood, I vow it will be memorable nonetheless. That small taste of her was not enough.

I take her hand in mine and promise to her, without words, that she will not regret this day. My cheeks hurt from smiling by the time the Elderman finishes the requisite prayers. I want this. But does she? Or is Reyne marrying me out of the same duty that brought me to her?

"Repeat my words, Lord Stokerton."

So I do.

"I take thee, Lady Reyne, to be my wedded wife, to have and to hold from this day forward." Reyne's eyes look wide and nervous. "For better or for worse, for fairer or fouler, to love and to cherish, till death us depart. According to God's holy ordinance, and thereunto I plight thee my troth."

Reyne, her voice more hesitant than I'd wish it to be, repeats the words, and we are proclaimed husband and wife.

Cheers erupt in the hall. I am pulled from Reyne almost immediately, embraced by Gille and my squire too. Hand grabbed and shaken by my new brother and father-in-law, and then the men who serve them. It is not until the hall has cleared out, save for about fifty people, and the trestle tables are pulled from the walls, that I am reunited with Reyne once more.

Not Lady Reyne, I remind myself, but my wife.

"Is that typical?" she asks as we are seated at a table for the two of us alone. As is customary, we are placed just below the dais and off to the side. And though many people are gazing at us with open curiosity, we can at last speak with each other. "To be pulled away after the ceremony as we were? I've not seen that before."

Our trenchers and goblets are filled, and the host and hostess make a toast that once again interrupts our conversation. All seem in good spirits, which is as it should be at a wedding. Even one that was conceived of just a few weeks earlier and planned in less than a day. Reyne slept here in the keep last eve. Bathed, her hair pulled back from her face by two braided strands, she looks as refreshed as I feel after a long dip in the river this morn. The same one we will need to cross as we head back to the capital.

As we toast, our eyes meet. A wave of desire surges through me. Which reminds me.

"Our wedding night," I say, lowering my voice, "should

not be in a tent. If we leave just after the meal, we can make Rymerden by sunset."

Lips slightly parted, my wife is, I hope, remembering the kisses we've shared. I've so much more to teach her. So much more for us to explore with each other.

And a lifetime to do it. Though I'd prefer not to wait quite so long.

"I'd have hoped," she pauses. "I'd have hoped to speak with my mother, or even my maid, before a wedding night I'm little prepared for."

I'd thought of that as well.

"We are husband and wife. There is naught you cannot ask me, naught you need be shy to say"—I smile—"or do with me. This night or any other. Do you understand?"

It is not the same, I realize that. But I will have to do, as both her husband and her confidant.

She nods.

"But first I must tell you." The look on her face reminds me that the boldness of her youth has largely been stolen from her, replaced with a fear I wish I could take away. "There are two river crossings, as there were on your way here, and another which is bridged. I will be by your side each time. You may ride with me, or on your own if you'd like. You will be safe, Reyne. I give you my word."

Although she licks her lips in distraction, not as an enticement, I cannot help but stare, growing more and more uncomfortable with each passing moment. There's no help for it but to look away, and to bide my time until this eve.

When Reyne becomes my wife in every way.

21

REYNE

*H*ow is it possible I am here, in a bedchamber of a castle I've never heard of before, in a place I never knew existed, waiting for a man who is now my husband?

Was it just this morn I walked into the great hall at Ledenhill and said the vows that saw me wed? After bidding goodbye to Warin and my father, who promised to send my belongings to Breywood Castle, we set off for Rymerden. Everything is moving impossibly fast, but Erik promised we will return home to see Mother as soon as it is safe.

After the wedding, we had a long day of travel, punctuated by a terrifying river crossing that had me clinging to Erik. Once we arrived, the maid who was sent to help me was kind enough to have a bath drawn, but that was long ago.

I expected Erik long before now.

The bedchamber is pleasant enough—decorated with two large blue wall coverings bearing the Tree of Loigh and an overly large, ominous-looking bed—but is nevertheless as foreign as the one I slept in last eve.

Nothing since I've left Blackwell has felt familiar. Perhaps that is the nature of marriage, of tying your life to someone outside of your home. It is to be expected, I suppose, but it is jarring nonetheless.

The door opens, and Erik enters just as I place my wooden brush back into the trunk along with my other belongings. It is the first time we have been alone all day, and even in the candlelight I can see he is glad for it.

Before I can utter a word, Erik strides toward me. He does not pause before hauling me to him, his head swooping down to mine. My lips open of their own accord, and just as he did before, all those days ago, he persuades me to open for him with his tongue. I have fretted over this decision a thousand times in the last few days, but every last doubt flees with his kiss.

I can feel his desire. His hips press to mine as a flutter in my stomach moves lower. Erik groans, his hands suddenly everywhere. At first, they are pressed flat against my back. But then one moves toward my waist, grasping the material there before sliding up the front of my shift.

His hand covers my breast, his skillful thumb rubbing my nipple through the material until it peaks. Through it all, he is kissing me, claiming my mouth. Already he is making my body answer to a new master, one I never expected to want or need.

Desire, full and fierce, encompasses every bit of me. I grip the material of his shirt with both hands, fisting it tightly as he continues his exploration. The kiss is like a dance. It started slowly, growing in confidence, and now there is no thinking. No hesitation.

I am engulfed in his embrace and enjoying each and every moment.

When Erik pulls away, his lips wet and his breath uneven,

I marvel at the thought that I did that to him. This champion of the Tournament of Loigh and commander to a queen is as beholden to me as I am to him in this moment.

"I've longed to kiss you that way," he says, lowering his head to my neck this time. Erik moves my hair to give himself greater access. "To feel you." He presses his lips to the sensitive flesh there. "To make you mine in every way." His kiss drifts toward the back of my ear. "You are so beautiful, Reyne."

He stops and stands tall, my arms having to reach high to continue to cling to him.

"Apologies," he says, "for my delay in coming tonight. I've learned some interesting news."

Erik's second hand follows the other's lead, and now both breasts receive equal treatment.

"Aye?" I manage as my hands slip to his shoulders. Erik steps back just slightly. When he looks down to his hands, still cupping my breasts, and smiles, my core clenches again. My body is preparing for him.

"The lord here is a distant cousin to the queen."

I attempt to ignore the twinge in my chest at his mention of her.

"He says sentiment begins to change, to be swayed in her favor. It appears she is not alone in wanting to explore peace despite the king's intent in sending the Oryan."

Hating how I feel when Erik talks of the queen, I concentrate on his hands as they move from my breasts downward, reaching behind me, cupping my buttocks and pulling me closer.

I never knew until this moment I wanted a man to grab me there.

"That is good," I manage. "You will need more than just the Highlanders' support, aye?"

He called me beautiful, but I would say the same of Erik's smile.

"Aye. Cettina will be pleased to hear it."

His smile falters.

"Reyne . . ." His hands freeze. "Your demeanor changes every time I say her name."

"Does it? I'd not noticed."

Liar.

"You are my wife."

"Because my father willed it," I cannot help but say. The thought has not been far from my mind this whole day.

"And because I willed it too. I'd not have agreed to his terms had the idea not appealed to me."

He's said as much, and yet still I wonder. "Nay? Not even for his support with the Highland Council?"

Would you not do anything for the queen?

I already know the answer, but I keep the question to myself, not wanting to ruin our wedding night.

"I'd not have agreed to his terms had I not wished to marry you, Reyne," he repeats. "And that was before we became reacquainted. I am happy to be married to you. Do you not sense that?"

I do, but . . .

"Cettina," he concludes.

I've not met her, but that does not prevent me from imagining the queen, whom he and others have described as a rare beauty, kissing my now husband. He does not love her in that way, I remind myself.

But neither does he love you.

Erik drops his hands, sighing.

"You do not believe me," he says more than asks. "You think me madly in love with Queen Cettina, and what? That we will engage in a salacious affair the moment we return to court?"

Precisely.

"Nay, but so many believe that."

"And so many are wrong. They know not the intricacies of our relationship. There will always be gossip at court, Reyne. I should have better prepared you for that. Many have little to do with their time other than speculate on others' lives. It makes them feel as if they've a measure of control. You'd do well to ignore it."

"I will try," I vow.

He is still studying me, but his look has changed from desire to concern. I hate that it's so, but I cannot change my thoughts.

Or can I?

Lady Arabelle pops into my mind then. She is right, *I* am his wife, not Queen Cettina. And Erik is worth fighting for.

"I will try," I say again more forcefully.

But my comment does not abate his concern. Brow furrowed, he says, "I do not wish for our first time together to be marred by your doubts."

I do not wish it either, but it seems it is too late.

Erik runs a hand through his hair. What is he thinking?

"I've upset you," I say.

"Nay, Reyne. You could never upset me by being honest. 'Tis all I ask from you. And I will give you the same in return."

Neither of us has moved, but the distance between us has grown.

I nod. "I gladly give it."

He looks pained. "Do you wish me as your husband?"

How could he ask such a question?

"Of course! We would not be married otherwise," I say, incredulous. It is I who was forced on him, not the other way around.

139

"Do you believe that I do not love Cettina? In the way that matters, as a husband loves a wife?"

Oh dear. This time, his questions are not so easy to answer. But I fear my silence has given me away.

I wish I could believe such a thing. But he has admitted to loving her, in a way. He's admitted to turning to her in a time of need. Clearly she means a great deal to him.

He frowns. "Can you give yourself to me without distraction? Without such thoughts swirling in your head?"

This one I can answer. I shake my head.

Erik closes his eyes. I lay my hands on his chest, forcing his eyes back open.

"You asked that I be honest."

His smile is sadder than I would have hoped for on our wedding night, but he has an intent look in his eyes, much like he did before the Triumph match.

"Despite how we came together, I am glad to be your husband." His hands cover mine.

"There is nothing I would rather do than pull that shift over your head and make love to you. Consummate our marriage as many times as you are able to given our long journey this day." He squeezes my hands. "But I cannot make you believe it, Reyne. I can only seek to prove it to you. I will prove it by denying myself the thing I want most this night, and on every night of this journey. I will continue to deny it when we reach Breywood if you are still not ready to give yourself to me without questioning whether I'm worthy of such a gift."

"You are more than worthy," I begin, but he stops me.

"I see the shadow that crosses your face at every mention of the queen," he says, moving our clasped hands over my heart. "I would dispel it if I could."

Then do so, I wish to say. *Tell me you love me, Erik, and we can share that very thing right now.*

Because in that moment, I realize it's true. I *do* love him.

But I can't bring myself to say any of that, so I simply sit there, uncertain, blinking up at him.

"I serve the queen," he says, and I can actually feel myself flinching. "You will speak with her. Dine with her. Cettina will be a part of our lives for many years. The only escape will be if I step down, which I can do at any time but am not willing to with Edingham's future so uncertain. You understand that, do you not?"

"Aye," I admit.

"Then we will come to a place where you no longer feel as you do. In the meantime." He lets go of my hands and wraps his arms around me. "We will become accustomed to each other. I will answer any questions you may have and be truthful always. And when you are ready—" This last part he murmurs in my ear, and I can hear the pain in his voice. "—when you are ready, tell me so."

My head, pressed up against his hard chest, begins to throb as the all too familiar feeling of an oncoming headache invades this doomed wedding night. I can tell him I'm ready this very moment. Confess that I've fallen in love with him, even as I've willed myself to keep my distance.

But perhaps Erik's idea has merit. Should we wait to mark this momentous occasion when Queen Cettina no longer casts a shadow on an otherwise bright beginning?

Perhaps.

Only . . . what if her shadow is everlasting? What will become of us then?

Without an answer, I allow myself to be held by a husband who did not ask for me but sacrifices for me even now. And that is something, is it not? Because I know what the evidence of his need feels like against me. There is no doubt this is a sacrifice for him.

The question is, how long will Erik be willing to wait if

I'm unable to overcome my jealousy of the queen? Mayhap it'll go away once I meet her. I will no longer have such feelings, and we can enjoy a glorious wedding night as soon as we reach Breywood.

Mayhap.

22

ERIK

*W*e ride through the gates of Breywood Castle, Bradyn jumping from his mount first. As he rushes forward to greet a young girl he fancies, the baker's daughter, I'm reminded that in many respects he is still a boy.

But fast becoming a man.

Other than a few mishaps, he did remarkably well on this trip.

Just as we ride through the gatehouse and outer curtain wall, onlookers gather around to watch. From our brief stop in the village, it seems word of Reyne has reached the castle ahead of us.

I attempted to prepare her for it, but my wife's mount slows beside me in a way that suggests she is hesitant. The more time I spend with Reyne, the more I can see the impact of her sister's death. One way she chooses to keep her sister alive is by pursuing her interests. Fara loved to read, and so that seems to be Reyne's current passion. She also has many new worries, I've found, most of them sparked by what she saw and experienced, by the loss she carries with her. I cannot pretend to understand what it is like to have a sibling, let alone lose one, but I wish to learn everything I can about Reyne . . . from her grief and worries to the fierce side of her I remember from childhood, for that girl is still a part of her too.

One day, just before reaching a river crossing, she spotted a deer in the distance. When she reached for the bow hanging from her saddle, I watched in fascination.

Reyne held her hand up in the air, signaling for silence, and then grabbed an arrow from the quiver. It was the first time I'd seen her touch the bow, which I'd meant to ask about.

The deer, still visible but well over three hundred paces away, moved just before she released the arrow. It would have been a near-impossible shot, but that she not only knew how to shoot and even attempted it, on horseback, had all three of us staring at her.

Reyne smiled at us and shrugged as she replaced the bow. "'Twas worth a try. We could have had a more resplendent supper this night."

Later, as we feasted by the fire on rabbit, I asked about her skill with the bow. Warin had apparently taught both of the sisters how to shoot. She claimed to have more accurate aim than even her brother, a claim I am eager to test in the yard. Imagining myself standing behind her, watching her backside as she draws back to shoot . . . it has become a common source of torture.

But there are plenty of others.

Lying with her in the tent. Enduring the hungry gazes she doesn't think I notice. One morn, upon waking, I found my hand firmly cupping a breast when I woke.

Sighing, I remind myself who is to blame for my own frustration as I watch Reyne dismount from her horse with the help of a stable boy.

Aye, I would know my wife in every way, but at this

particular moment, stopping an attack and avoiding war takes precedence. As I hand off my reins, I ask Bradyn to run ahead to tell Cettina we've arrived. She likely already knows we are here, but I need an immediate audience.

Reyne is nervous, as am I. I hate that the queen has come between us and wonder if meeting her will make matters better, or worse. I suppose we will soon find out.

"It is magnificent," Reyne says softly.

Situated on a wooded bend along the Hebanby River, too far south to be considered part of the Highlands but far enough from the border to be safe from the entanglements that have plagued Edingham since it became independent from Meria, Breywood Castle *is* magnificent. Still, it is modest for the seat of kings and queens.

"Shall I find you an escort to our rooms, or would you accompany me directly to the queen?" I ask as Reyne takes my arm. We're remarkably comfortable with each other for a pair of former neighbors who hadn't seen each other for more than ten years. Even Gille has commented on it. If only we could consummate the marriage . . .

"I would remain with you," she says.

Gille and I exchange a glance. He knows of her hesitation to meet the queen, something she's mentioned to him herself. If only he knew the extent of that hesitation. I have told no one about our arrangement, nor do I intend to do so.

"Then come," I say, greeting well-wishers and thanking them as we make our way through the courtyard and up a flight of stone stairs that leads straight to the entrance for the great hall. Though we do not step inside, Reyne pauses for a moment.

"'Tis a lovely hall," she says. "So much color."

Indeed, the crests of each king of Edingham hang from every corner, one more colorful than the last. And with the trestle tables pushed up against the walls, it appears bigger now than it does during mealtimes.

"The lady's chamber is this way," I say as we walk toward what was once called the lord's chamber, just to the right of the great hall. Because the queen spends much of her time in here, two guards stand at its entrance. They glance at Reyne but say nothing.

"She's waiting for me?"

Their presence confirms Cettina is inside, and Bradyn's message would have arrived by now.

"Aye," says Alan, third son of a minor Highland lord.

Pausing before we enter, I lean down and kiss Reyne on the cheek, not knowing precisely what to say to calm her fears. I nod, and the double doors are pulled open by the guards.

The lady's chamber is not overly large, although it boasts two sizeable windows, each with plush velvet window seats. The shutters are thrown open at present, allowing in fresh air. Cettina sits behind an enormous oak desk not meant to be moved, unlike most of the furniture in this castle. Built by her great-grandfather, it is meant to intimidate, and for most people it does.

I squeeze Reyne's arm, then release it so I can bow to the queen. My wife follows suit. A quick glance reveals she's discomfited, but there's naught I can do to reassure her. So I take her arm and present her to the queen.

"May I present my wife, Lady Reyne, daughter of Lord Moray of Blackwell."

Cettina would know of my marriage by now from the message I'd sent.

"Reyne, this is Queen Cettina Borea, first of her name, sovereign of the great kingdom of Edingham."

Cettina speaks first, as etiquette dictates.

"Lady Reyne," she says, "I am pleased to welcome you to Breywood Castle. And I congratulate you on your marriage."

She turns to me.

"'Twas a most surprising, though not unpleasant, bit of news to learn you'd married, Lord Stokerton."

Though I don't look at Reyne, I can feel her tense beside me.

Perhaps not so surprising as you tasked me with gaining Lord Moray's support with the Highland Council. Of course, I don't voice the thought aloud.

Cettina's brows rise.

"And to Lord Moray's daughter?" There's something harsh in her tone, and the words are clipped in a way that indicates she is not pleased at all.

"Aye."

She turns to Reyne, opens her mouth, and closes it. Whatever words she struggled with are forgotten, and she says instead, "We've much to discuss, Erik."

I wince at her use of my given name. I don't need to glance at Reyne to know this is not going well.

"Aye," I agree. "I bring news of an urgent matter."

She looks back at me.

"More urgent than the news you traveled to Ledenhill for?"

"Aye."

She frowns. "I've news as well, from Meria. But our discussion can wait."

Aye, she is definitely angry—her tone leaves little room for doubt. But why? Could she be jealous after all, and I've misread all that's passed between us?

"First I wish to speak to your wife. Alone."

I place my right hand on Reyne's wrist, which is tucked through my arm, defying my queen on her behalf sooner than I would have liked.

147

"She is new to court, and I would prefer to stay with her," I say, as sternly as I dare. "If it pleases you."

Cettina looks back and forth between us.

"It does not please me."

Something is amiss. This is not the Cettina I know, and I will not leave Reyne alone with her.

But my wife's fierce side makes another appearance, and she lifts my hand and disengages her arm.

"We will do as the queen bids," she says, as if she has experience navigating the whims of royalty. Her eyes implore me to do as she asks. Hesitant, I relent only when she more forcefully pushes me away.

"Go," she says. "I will join you shortly."

With a final glance at the queen, I reluctantly bow and turn to leave.

Uneasy, uncertain, and very much aware our marital celibacy will not end this night as I'd dared to hope, I knock and the doors are opened.

This does not bode well at all.

23

REYNE

*E*rik and I will never consummate our marriage.

If the act hinges on my heart being free of uncertainty about Queen Cettina, I should pack my belongings this very day and leave for home. Or at least resolve not to have the kind of marriage I've hoped for these past days.

Sitting before me is the most beautiful woman I've ever met. Nay, not only beautiful, but self-assured as well. As she spoke with Erik, each word fell from her lips like an arrow, quick and sure. It left me feeling like I always do at river crossings. Although I no longer break out in tears anymore, my hands still shake. My heart still pounds with visions of the current carrying me away.

The queen stands now, her hair the color of straw, but brighter and glossier, a silver circlet around the top of her head. She looks younger than I expected, no older than I am, but also much, much wiser, as if she's lived many lifetimes.

The queen's face is kissed by the sun, with smooth cheeks and perfectly formed brows. In short, she is . . . perfection. And seemingly very unhappy about my marriage to Erik. She walks toward me now, head held high, but I stand tall.

As she approaches, her scent wafts toward me. The sweet smell of berries, something I hadn't expected. Something in me quails, but I force myself to imagine my father, defiant and proud. He allows nothing to sway him. Whether he is right or wrong, he always acts with complete conviction, which can be a curse as often as it is a blessing. But in this moment, I need his confidence.

I am Lord Moray's daughter, and I will not cower.

She stops.

"I bid Stokerton to gain the Highlanders' support, and he returns with a bride. How did this come to be?"

Why is she not asking Erik that very question?

"My father saw an opportunity in Lord Stokerton's request. To ally our families. To see me married, finally."

Her eyes flash in anger. Does she love my husband after all?

"Was this marriage against your will?"

"Nay," I say as forcefully as I am able.

Her shoulders sag, her eyes close. Her reaction is so surprising, I know not what to do. Or say. So I just fold my hands in front of me and wait.

Her eyes open, considerably softer than before.

"When I heard about your marriage, I feared . . . Erik would do anything for Edingham."

For the first time since I came into this chamber, the queen smiles. A broad smile that appears so genuine, I am taken aback.

"You willed it, then?" she asks again.

I'd assumed she was angry Erik had married. Could it have been concern rather than anger?

"I did," I say, my hands still folded together. "I knew him when we were young, before our fathers stopped speaking. Our joining was my decision. My father told Erik we could not wed without my permission."

She appears more than a little surprised.

"Your father is indulgent."

"Aye. After my younger sister died, he became even more so."

A shadow crosses her face, and then I remember she lost, and regained, a sister too. If only I could bring Fara back.

The queen shocks me again when she steps forward and reaches for my hands.

"I am glad for it, then. I'd have preferred not to have your father's support if it came at the cost of a forced marriage. But if you've chosen Erik as your husband," she says, still smiling, "then I shall not have him tossed in the dungeon after all."

She has not yet released my hands, and it is an odd feeling indeed, to find the woman who's caused me so much distress to be so kind and accommodating.

"Welcome to court," she says. "May I call you Reyne?"

As if I would deny a queen.

"Aye."

"In private you have leave to call me Cettina, as Erik does. I trust none as much as him, and I would very much like to have another confidant here at court."

"Surely you must have many," I blurt out. "The Curia, your ladies, your . . ." I stop just before saying *sister*.

The queen releases my hands and walks toward a cushioned trunk, gesturing for me to sit on another opposite it.

"My sister," she guesses, quite correctly, "travels with her husband."

I wince inwardly, knowing Erik's news will complicate what is, for her, already a fraught relationship with her sister's husband. He will need to be punished, just like the rest of the traitors.

"Erik is the only member of the Curia not chosen by my

151

father. Some are loyal to me, others—" she shrugs, "—in time will be replaced."

I gasp aloud before stopping myself. Such a thing is not done. The chancellor, commanders, and justiciary of the Curia are lifelong positions unless they choose otherwise. Even more surprising is that she would openly tell me such a thing. On our very first meeting.

"As for my ladies?" The twinkle in the queen's eyes can only be described as mischievous. "There is but one who wants nothing of me other than my love. She is a dear friend, and one I will introduce you to straightaway. The others . . ." She rolls her eyes. "All placed by my side for a specific purpose. Some by my father's friends, and others by me. But not because I fully trust their or their families' intentions."

I don't know what to say.

She is surrounded by people she does not love or trust. What must that be like?

"I met your father once," she says. "I remember him clearly."

No longer peeved at him, I think of my father fondly, missing him even now. I smile, imagining him at court. He would hate it. "That must have been many years ago?"

She nods. "Aye, I was but a child. I remember asking my maid why his hair was so red. I'd never seen such a shade of hair before."

Laughing, I inadvertently reach up to my own hair. "We had that in common, before his turned grey," I say.

"I did not speak to him, but he smiled at me as he walked by. And as I'd done many times, with many men, I secretly wished to have him as a father. You see, mine did not smile. Not at me, at least."

From what I've heard of King Malcom, that does not surprise me.

"He is a good father," I say. "Kind and loving, in his own way. But he is not perfect."

"I've yet to meet a man or woman alive who can claim such a thing."

"Perfection?" I think of Erik. He is close. But I am not the only one tormented by ghosts.

"You think of your husband." She smiles knowingly. "I should ask him back. It seems he has important news?"

"I will fetch him," I say, standing. A day ago, I would never have dreamed I would be willingly bringing Erik to the queen, for any purpose, but I feel differently after meeting her. Despite the fact that the queen is indeed as beautiful, regal, and fierce as everyone whispers her to be, I am less afraid.

She is exactly as Erik has described, and if Cettina is offering friendship, I shall take it.

"And I gladly accept your offer . . . Cettina."

"I am glad, Reyne."

I step back, bow, and bid her adieu.

With a final glance at Queen Cettina, I knock on the wooden doors of her chamber and wait as they creak open.

24

ERIK

"We learned of it by chance, Reyne's brother having overheard a conversation that led us there."

Despite the importance of this discussion, I cannot help but think of the look Reyne gave me outside the chamber. She was worried.

The entire time she was in here, speaking with Cettina, I paced back and forth in front of the door and imagined all manner of scenarios.

Most of them ended with my wife being unhappy. It wasn't until I spoke to Cettina myself that I understood the nature of her concern. Having spent much of her life beholden to the whims of her tyrannical father, Cettina has little tolerance for men who force their will upon women, in any manner. I wish she hadn't thought the worst of me—I would never have forced an unwilling bride to the altar—but I'm relieved she was concerned for my wife.

My wife. I'm desperate to speak to her, but it will have to wait. Before this meeting with Cettina, I arranged for Reyne to be brought to our rooms and assigned a maid, so at least she will be comfortable.

After reassuring Cettina that Moray would indeed urge the Highland Council to stand down, I started to explain what we had learned.

"It appears the attack on Saitford was carried out not by Borderers but"—my fists clench into balls at my side—"by those wishing to incite a war with Meria."

Cettina, seated once again behind her desk, frowns.

"Who?"

"Lord Rawlins," I say. Her scowl deepens, for we both know him to be a traitorous bastard. "And your brother-in-law . . . I saw him enter the dovecote."

As the news penetrates, Cettina's shoulders rise and fall. Though she is angry, no doubt, this cannot come as a surprise. Whitley is the worst sort of man, one Cettina has loathed since her father first forced Lady Hilla to marry him. Marriage to a king's daughter had completed his family's rise to prominence, the coup Whitley himself had never failed to flout.

Until the affair.

Being cast out of court in such a way was the gravest possible insult, and his anger toward Hilla is palpable whenever I'm in their presence. Whether or not Lady Hilla did indeed have an affair with Lord Bowes, I can only speculate on. Cettina will not discuss her sister, and even though they have now been welcomed back at court, they do not reside here and I rarely see them.

"Hilla is with him," she says quietly.

I was afraid that might be so. Hilla herself told Cettina that Lord Whitley no longer lets her out of his sight. Still, she refuses to leave him, even though her sister has begged her to do so and promised to grant her a divorce.

"There is more dire news than that," I continue. "We were

set upon in the woods by a man named Father Aiken. I believe he is a Shadow Warrior."

Cettina has even less love for the Prima than she does her brother-in-law, and her expression says as much.

"He claims to be a spy."

She looks doubtful, which I was as well.

"He could have harmed us," I admit. "None of us saw him approach. I chose to trust him, and the man did indeed give us solid information. He said a repeat of Saitford will occur in one month's time, so less than a fortnight from now, at Firley Dinch."

Springing from her seat, just as I expected she might, Cettina asks, "Do you believe him?"

"Could it be a trap? Aye. But we've no choice but to respond."

Though Firley Dinch is just a four-day ride from Breywood, we need time to prepare.

"If the Elderman is honest, they will not know we're coming. He claims less than thirty men will carry out the attack. Unmarked, as they were before. They will meet at dawn in ten days' time outside Craighcebor."

A small village situated on the bank of the Terese River, just across the bridge from Firley Dinch, Craighcebor is both wealthy from trade and ravaged by constant skirmishes with the Merian Borderers.

"Assemble the Curia," she says, unaware that I've done so already, anticipating her response. They are likely either outside the doors or on their way here.

"You will lead a force to Craighcebor, and I am coming."

She holds up a hand as I start to object.

"My sister is there," she says. "And we will send word to King Galfrid as well, to warn him of the attack. He will not have time to send men, but I would have him know this court is not complicit. If we are somehow unsuccessful in stopping them, I fear Rawlins and Whitley's aim will find its target. Another Saitford will spark the very war we've worked so hard to avoid. And he should know the extent of the Prima's interference as it does not bode well for either kingdom."

Though I agree with Cettina's assessment, her plan is not without risks. If the Elderman is indeed setting a trap, warning the Merian king could cause more trouble than it averts. And little would I blame him. Two attacks such as Saitford against Edingham, and we would already be assembling an army against Meria.

There is no reason to think Galfrid would not do the same.

"This Elderman," Cettina says, "will either help us prevent a war, or start one."

I think of Father Aiken's deadly glare.

"Aye," I agree. And at this moment, I cannot say for certain which is the more likely outcome.

"*We* leave tomorrow."

I'd hoped for at least a few more days at the castle to help Reyne become accustomed to Breywood, but fewer risks can be taken since Cettina has chosen to travel with Lord Scott and I to the border. The decision was made to leave in the morn so our men have time to firmly install themselves at Carwell Castle in Craighcebor.

Reyne looks different with her hair piled atop her head. Her belongings will not arrive for some time, but her new maid somehow procured two new gowns for her. She's wearing one of them now, dressed for supper in a cream gown with long, open sleeves lined with gold thread, her hair in stark contrast. She is so very lovely, and the thought of leaving her so soon makes me ache inside.

"So soon," she says, dejected. A sentiment I can understand.

"Aye." I stroll to a bowl of scented water left by the chambermaid. Tugging out of my surcoat, I am about to pull my shirt up to wash when Reyne's look stops me.

"I'm not accustomed to sharing my chamber," I say,

although truthfully I'm pleased to do so. Reyne is like the first bright flower to bloom in a field that has seen the ravages of winter. Since Isolda, I've shied away from the thought of marriage, necessary though I knew it would be someday, and yet, here she is, looking at me with a mixture of distress and . . . something more.

"I'm glad you are here," I clarify, taking off the shirt and positioning myself over the bowl. It's only after I've rinsed, when I pick up the drying cloth to wipe my face, that I notice Reyne is staring.

She has seen me shirtless before, on our travels, but never under these circumstances. Never alone in a room with a large bed.

"Tell me of your meeting," I say, immediately regretting my words. It is silly of me to think, hope, that her fears might have been eradicated by a single discussion with the queen.

Reyne sits on the bed, and although she's been up here for a while now, I catch her glancing about the chamber. I'm suddenly grateful to have been assigned such well-appointed rooms. Once occupied by Cettina's mother, they were designed for comfort, with velvet-cushioned window seats and the large canopied bed on which Reyne sits. This circular tower is thankfully at the opposite end of the castle and the river, but if it were not, I'd have arranged for us to move. Brightly colored trunks and cupboards that hold all manner of things, from bowls for washing to books that were here when I arrived, line the chamber. A sitting room is attached, one I hardly use and will gladly give up to Reyne.

Hopefully not for sleeping, however. Unlike some married couples, I plan for her to be in my bed, or our bed, each night.

"She was exactly as you described her," Reyne says, her appreciative gaze not lost on me, particularly not on that part of me which is difficult to tame at the moment.

I splash more cold water on my face. One can never be too clean. When I dry myself again, Reyne doesn't seem to realize anything is amiss.

"At first I was afraid. She seemed angry that we'd wed."

"Aye," I agree. "She was angry, at me."

Reyne nods. "I realized that, but only after I'd finished being terrified. She has the demeanor of someone twice her age."

"A result of being the sole woman in a court of men."

"I do not envy her, Erik. She told me she is eager to become friends because she lacks true ones here at court."

Fully dried, I move toward a trunk to retrieve a fresh linen shirt.

"She told you that?"

"Aye."

I pull one out, shake it, and am about to pull it over my head. But Reyne stops me with a look.

Almost as if . . .

Tossing the shirt back onto the trunk, I hold her gaze.

"You've won the queen over in one meeting," I say honestly. "She'd not have said that otherwise."

Reyne's lips part.

I don't waste another moment. Though I don't wish to ruin her hair or dress, I cannot resist my wife. Sitting down next to her, I pull her head toward mine. I'm more than ready for her to become my wife in truth—indeed, the strain of not doing so is nearly killing me—but I've vowed to wait for Reyne to tell me she's ready.

So instead of ravishing her, as I would like, I coax her lips open and touch my tongue to hers. The sweetness of her quickly overwhelms my good intentions. Very much aware we sit on the precipice of another lesson, as I anxiously await Reyne's permission to show her how much more pleasure awaits us, I move from her lips downward.

Lower, and lower still, until I'm all but buried between her breasts. There, I grow bolder than I should, kissing both and plunging my fingers inside her décolletage. The dress is low-cut enough for me to reach her nipple, and I caress it as Reyne grips my bare shoulder.

Growing hard, but determined not to continue until she wills it, I lift my head and look into her eyes. Uncertainty. Desire. Caring.

I wonder what she sees in me?

"Reyne," I begin, knowing this is the last night we will be together. "We can dine in the hall as planned, or we can eat here. I'll have food brought to us, if you'd like."

"You are not expected in the hall?"

"Nay," I assure her. "I am not."

"But as commander, I just thought . . . are there not plans to be made for the morrow?"

That she seems eager to stay encourages me, though I remind myself she is agreeing to dine here, nothing more.

As of yet.

"The plans have been made." My errant hand finally drops to her lap, though it itches to feel more. Explore more. "We leave at dawn for Carwell Castle in Craighcebor. Scouts will move ahead of us to prepare the Lord of Carwell for our arrival. Once there, we will lie low until Whitley and Rawlins surface. We've sent word to King Galfrid as well."

As expected, Reyne is surprised by that news.

"You truly believe this Shadow Warrior tells the truth?"

God, I wish I knew the answer to that question.

"If he does not, we should be able to root out an ambush. Either way, the king will know our interest in peace is sincere."

"I heard some talk of King Galfrid's nephew gaining support as his replacement heir. They say he is now officially backed by the church?"

"One of many, many rumors you will hear circulating here at court. But aye, that one is true enough. And by Father Aiken's own words, the Prima was involved at Saitford and this attack as well. Which means Father Silvester is as complicit as anyone."

How did we get so far astray from more important matters? I'd prefer to turn the discussion back to us, to our marriage, and I also do not want Reyne to worry. "We will stop the attack, expose both Whitley and Rawlins, and reopen the path to peace."

"What will happen to them?"

The Curia discussed that as well.

"Both will be arrested, and likely hung, as traitors."

"Whitley too?"

I nod. "Aye, Whitley too. Cettina is hoping to discover her sister's whereabouts before the fighting."

Reyne noticeably tenses. "Cettina?"

"She is coming to Craighcebor. We tried to dissuade her, but knowing Lady Hilla travels with her husband, she insists on being there. Which is one of the reasons we chose Carwell Castle. It is as fortified as any castle, more so after so often being ravaged by Borderers."

I stop, seeing her expression.

Reyne is no longer looking at me with appreciation, as if she would very much like to remain in this chamber, as I would, until dawn. She's tense suddenly. Withdrawn.

"You met her," I say. "Surely you know now there is nothing more between Cettina and I than respect and mutual admiration. She trusts me, as she always has. I just ask that you do the same for me."

Reyne says nothing. I stand, frustrated at this turn of events.

"Why do you think so poorly of me, Reyne? Have I given you cause to do so?"

She makes a face nearly identical to one I've seen before. On her father.

"I was thrust upon you, Erik. And she is . . ." She purses her lips together and does not finish the thought. "I shall go with you."

"No."

Not the right answer.

"It is too dangerous. We go there to fight a battle, Reyne. Mayhap one we are not as prepared for as we believe. I would not see harm come to you. Nay, you will remain here."

I've been looking for the fire in her eyes.

I see it now . . . directed at *me*.

"But it is safe enough for Cettina?"

"I'd not have her come either, but she is the queen and wills it so."

"And I am naught but your wife, so you may tell me what to do." She stands and mutters, "Just like my father."

My only thought is to keep my wife safe from harm. And she is angry because of it?

Stalking back to my shirt, I lift it over my head, then pull the surcoat on top of it. Running my hands through my hair, I wonder how a night that began with such promise could fall apart so swiftly.

"Shall we go to supper?" I say, my words clipped.

Without answering, Reyne walks toward the door and swings it open, waiting for me.

Aye, she and Cettina will get along quite well.

REYNE

*T*he very woman causing my current misery is watching me now. And though I'm attempting to converse with Lord Scott, the queen's first commander, and Gille, whom I've gotten to know fairly well on our travels, I cannot help but watch her as well.

On the dais above us, Cettina sits surrounded by her ladies. It is odd to see so many women up there. Often only a lord's wife and daughters would be seated so prominently. But here, there were no men on the dais at all.

Her father is dead. She has no uncles. As she told me earlier, she is in many ways quite alone in the world. And yet, she smiles easily. Eats and drinks with effortless grace. It is as if she were born for the role.

When I catch Erik watching me, I quickly look away.

Angry both with him and myself, I stab the meat on our shared trencher.

"'Tis already dead," Erik says.

Gille chuckles next to him. "You should join us, Lady Reyne, on our next hunt. You've clearly much skill with the bow."

Pleased someone at this table has noticed I am not some simpering maid, I thank him. "I will willingly accept your invitation."

The meal passes with few words between Erik and I. Then, without warning, the queen stands. She holds out her hand, apparently to indicate that all others in the hall may remain seated.

"Most often, when she is finished, the meal is officially over," Erik says, watching me. "Tonight she will apparently retire early."

As he explains, one of Cettina's ladies approaches us from behind.

"Lady Reyne?"

Both Erik and I turn to her.

"I am Lady Gwenllian. When you are finished with your meal, the queen would like to speak with you."

Erik seems less than pleased. For myself, I know not what to think. When I stand, Lady Gwenllian stops me.

"It is not necessary to leave now."

"I am finished," I say, standing. "Pardon me," I say to the others, "I bid you a good eve."

Erik moves to stand as well, but I stop him.

"There is no need for you to accompany me. Unless Queen Cettina wishes to speak with us both?"

Gwenllian shakes her head.

"Then I bid you a good eve as well, husband."

Following Lady Gwenllian from the hall, I do not spy the queen anywhere even though she left but a moment ago.

"She moves quickly," Gwenllian says, hiking her skirts up as we move past a set of guards and ascend the circular stone stairs behind the hall.

"This will take us to the upper chambers."

I am truly lost by the time we arrive in a long hall, again flanked by guards.

"The queen's private chambers are up here," she says. "Come."

We pass wall torches and at least five separate doors before stopping in front of the one at the end of the hallway. Gwenllian knocks, and the door is immediately opened by a maid. She moves to the side, and though I wait for my companion to join me, she does not.

"Queen Cettina asked for you alone," she says without hesitation, making me wonder if she is the dear friend the queen mentioned earlier.

"Go inside," she prompts, and I do.

Two additional maids are already assisting the queen as she undresses. One unties her gown at the back while the other stands in front of her, hands held out. Cettina is reaching into her hair, pulling out pins one by one and handing them to the maid.

"I did not expect you so soon," she says. "Come in."

Though the bedchamber is large, it is no bigger than my mother and father's back home. It is modest for a queen, although it is as opulently appointed as I would expect. A fire is already lit in the corner. Cettina nods to one of the two chairs next to it.

When I move to sit, the maid with the pins hands me a goblet. I accept, peering inside.

"I visited Sindridge once," Cettina says. "The region where that wine hails from." She steps out from the crimson gown, dressed now in a simple but fine undergown. Nodding to the maids and retrieving her own goblet from a cupboard against the wall, she joins me as the two women leave the chamber.

"Do you not find it a relief to be rid of such things?" she says, indicating her gown, now laid out atop the largest trunk I have ever seen. "Have you worn men's breeches before?"

Not knowing which question to answer first, I say "nay" to the breeches.

"I wear them in the training yard. They are quite freeing. 'Tis said the women in Murwood End wear them most days. But I confess, I've not been there for many years, so I cannot confirm that particular rumor. Although even as a child, I suspect I would have noticed women dressed as men."

Sipping wine by the fire and listening to her, I can almost forget this woman is the queen.

"I've never been to Murwood End," I confess. "My father says they do not welcome Highlanders."

"Hmm. They do not welcome most anyone who is not native to Murwood End. Did Erik tell you he traveled there not long ago?"

"Aye. He said the king's commander was there at the same time."

"A man by the name of Lord Vanni d'Abella. The king's son who is not his son."

I've heard the name, but I know little of the man.

"They say he married a Garra from Murwood End. A woman he met on that very visit."

"A Garra," I repeat, almost whimsically. Although the woman who sold me the Kona pin is the only Garra I've ever seen, I've read all their teachings. "My sister loved to read. Our tutor procured many books, some teaching of the Garra. I think there is much to be learned from them."

Cettina takes a sip of her wine.

"There is much to be learned from everyone. Tell me of her. Your sister."

I do, sadness creeping into my voice more than once. And yet, I find myself recalling happy memories more and more lately, through the haze of grief. It makes me hopeful to think there will be a day when I can again think of Fara with joy.

CECELIA MECCA

Cettina says nothing of her own sister.

"You told me earlier that Erik did not force you to wed him," she says, abruptly changing the topic. "I see how he looks at you. And when you think he does not notice, how you look at him. So tell me, why do you let our past come between your present?"

I'm so startled by her question, I simply stare.

"I've spent a lifetime enduring looks of jealousy, of discerning others' thoughts sometimes before they say a word."

If a hole were to suddenly open beneath my seat, sending me tumbling to the very depths of the castle, it would please me greatly.

"Do you know my favorite thing to do?" she asks, and then, before I can answer, "I imagine how it must be to live as the person I'm speaking to. My maids. The Curia. My enemies. And you." She takes another sip. "I've thought of how I would feel had I arrived at the Tournament of Loigh thinking I would return home, only to fall for a man who is both glorious and complicated. To marry him, wondering the whole time if he cared more for me or his sense of duty and the task he'd been given by the queen he serves. And then to meet that very queen, knowing she once shared a kiss with the man who is now my husband."

My chest and face are aflame. Did she just say that aloud?

"And if I loved that man? I would feel lost and confused, excited at times but saddened at others. I would wonder how to forge a new life without having a chance to mourn my old one. I would feel further away from the sister I'd lost . . ."

The beginnings of tears sting my eyes.

"And confused by how to treat with a woman who is all at once a queen, a woman, a potential friend, and the person who stands between me and the happiness I'm unsure that I deserve."

I pull out the ever-present handkerchief in the pocket sewn into the side of my gown and dot both corners of my eyes. I cannot look at her just yet. My chest hurts, my eyes sting. Embarrassment would have me rushing from the room, yet I'm filled with a sense of awe that compels me to speak.

"How?" I ask, hoping she understands what I cannot put into words.

"'Tis not difficult," she says, "if one simply listens and imagines how they might feel in a similar situation. Listen, and love. Naught else matters."

The sentiment is so close to something Fara would have said.

"You've read the Garra's teachings," Cettina says, "and I too believe in the power of love."

Sipping the wine, I think on her words and realize they're true. All of them.

"As for that kiss, one I *know* Erik must have told you about, given the way you looked at me through supper . . ." She leans forward in her seat. "We knew immediately it was all wrong. Erik and I were both in a dark place, and we attempted to console ourselves. Your husband is quite handsome and kind, a combination that is sadly rare in men who wield any modicum of power. But there was not—" she waves her hand, "—the connection you share."

She smiles.

"He loves you, Reyne. I can see it clearly."

The goblet freezes on my lips.

"I know him as well as any man. He cared for Isolda, but he did not love her. He *does* love you."

I lower the goblet onto my lap after a lengthy sip, though I did not drain it down the way I did at Havefest.

"He will not allow me to travel with him tomorrow," I confess.

Cettina frowns.

"You wish to come?"

I think about it for a moment. And realize that, aye, I'd prefer to be there than to be like my mother, waiting for Father to return, not knowing when or even if he would.

"Aye. I wish to come."

She shrugs, as if it is not a problem at all.

"We leave at dawn. If you return to your chamber, Erik will see you rising with him in the morn. Stay here this night. I've an empty bedchamber just down the hall. We will send him word and then—" she smiles brightly, "—he will say nothing when you ride out with me in the morn."

I cannot. "Nay, it would not be proper to abandon him this night."

Cettina all but rolls her eyes. "You determine what is proper now. Not Erik. Not protocol. Not your father. You, Reyne. If you wish to come to Craighcebor, then come to Craighcebor. If you wish to stay behind, stay behind. If you allow others to dictate your life, then it is their life you live."

Could I do such a thing? *Should* I do such a thing? What will Erik think or say?

Suddenly it occurs to me, Cettina sits here advising me, helping me, when she rides out tomorrow to save her sister. To avoid a war for her kingdom. And yet she appears calm and relaxed, and I think I begin to understand the reason why.

If you allow others to dictate your life, then it is their life you live.

After my sister died, I honored her life by living as she would. These past weeks, I'm unsure whose life I've lived, precisely.

He loves you.

If her words are true, and I sense they are, then he will forgive me for living as myself in the days to come.

"I will do it," I say as Cettina smiles back. "But only if you allow me to borrow a pair of breeches."

Her laugh is a healing ointment to my battered soul.

ERIK

I should have expected as much.

When I received word Reyne was staying in the queen's rooms and she would see me off in the morn, I was not surprised. Cettina had whisked her away from supper for a reason. That reason, I supposed, had to do with our uncomfortable supper. And the queen was not the only one to have noticed the tension between us.

Gille asked me about it too, and I confessed to some of our difficulties. He had little advice to offer, except to reiterate that which he'd said once before. But I don't need anyone to tell me I'm different with Reyne. I know it. I feel it.

When I see her, with Reyne having said she would meet me in the courtyard this morn to see me off, I understand precisely what they were planning—for as Cettina rides toward me, wearing breeches and a surcoat with the Tree of Loigh prominent on her chest, a woman in an identical outfit rides beside her.

See me off indeed. When I catch my wife's eyes, she is unapologetic. Brazen, even.

My inclination is to laugh. This minx is every bit the girl

who hid under a trestle table in her father's hall to spy on a meeting. There's little I can say now, and she well knows it. Besides which, the riding party is fifty strong, and it is my duty to ride in front of the group, Lord Scott in back. Any more than fifty, we surmised, would be too difficult to hide well at Carwell Castle. Much of our plan hinges on the bastards planning this heinous attack not knowing we are there. Unless, of course, Father Aiken lied to us and we are being betrayed by him.

By staying at Carwell and not somewhere closer to the border of Firley Dinch, we've planned for such a circumstance. Thankfully, we will not be close to the fighting if any should occur, the only fact that consoles me about Reyne's presence.

It is only much later that I have occasion to look back for my wife. The stream is small, hardly notable, but I still mean to cross it with her.

She meets my eyes and shakes her head slightly, or so it seems from the distance.

Does she not want me to escort her across?

I wait as she and the queen approach the water, and now that she's closer, I can tell she is indeed waving me off. Because she is still angry? Aye, likely so. I ride ahead but feel compelled to turn once I reach the other bank so that I might watch her cross. Though it is but a stream, most of the rocks at the bottom visible, I hold my breath as she makes her way across. Relieved when she does it without hesitation, I ride back to the front.

All day, she rides with the queen.

We stop only once. Though I wish to speak with Reyne, I'm too stubborn to do so, and she clearly has no great wish to treat with me. It rankles that she does not trust me to make this journey alone, even more so because she does not appear to hold the situation against Cettina, only against me.

So even though my eyes are strained from trying so hard not to look back at her, I do not attempt to speak with her until we stop for the eve.

As the men set up the tents, the Curia having agreed it is too dangerous for us to stay anywhere well-traveled enough to boast an inn, I stride toward the two women. The only ones on this journey.

I shake my head at the irony of their newfound friendship. Even now the two are huddled together, laughing about something they see in the distance. Reyne points toward the trees as Cettina shakes her head.

Until I approach.

And then their laughter cuts off abruptly, as if I'd doused them both with a cold bucket of water.

"Lord Scott will see to camp," I say, my eyes drifting toward Reyne's long, lean legs as she stands. Her surcoat is much shorter than Cettina's, and it gives me a perfect view of them.

"You are hunting for supper?" Cettina guesses.

I lift the bow in my hand. "Always perceptive, my queen."

She makes a sound that some might interpret as a snort. Of course, she is a queen, and queens do not snort. Or so she's told me before.

"Reyne." I hardly know what to say to her. So many emotions roil through me. Anger, disappointment, worry and, as she stares definitely back at me, lust.

"Erik."

With nothing more to say, at least in front of Cettina and the others within hearing, I nod to both women and turn to leave.

Reyne does not stop me.

Four of us head out in opposite directions to hunt. Another two scouts have already ridden a good distance ahead to ensure our location is secure. As I make my way east, away from the clearing where we made camp, the deep thicket of woods becomes even thicker. There is enough light to hunt by for now, but it will soon fade away. If I do not catch something soon, it will be left to the others to provide the meal.

Stopping to listen carefully, the sound of running water is the only one I can hear. Walking toward it, I'm surprised when the trees clear once again and a small stream appears. Larger than the one we crossed earlier but not so large as to be listed on the map, I make my way toward its banks to look for tracks. Seeing small prints freshly cut into the mud, I stop and listen once again.

Still nothing.

Crouching down for a better look, I realize a deer is close by, either a small buck or large doe. The distance between the prints made by the front feet tells me this deer is walking and not running.

A good sign.

Following the trail along the riverbank, I mark enough time that I consider heading back. And then I hear it.

The crack of a twig sounds behind me. Turning, I see someone back where I'd first left the woods. As I make my way toward the figure, my hand on the hilt of the sword at my side, it becomes quickly apparent that the someone is a woman.

With flaming red hair.

Wearing men's breeches.

I break into a run as I see Reyne crouch down beside the water. Calling out her name, my heart thudding at the sight before me, I run faster. As if in a dream, she does not turn toward me. Instead, she reaches out, her hand dipping into the water.

"Reyne," I call out again. She knows I approach, anyone

175

trained to hunt as she has been would hear much quieter sounds, but still does not look my way. "Reyne."

What is she doing?

Finally, I reach my wife and see, for the first time, she is crying as she slips her fingers into the water. But not in a terrified way. It is sadness that grips her now, and a love that engulfs me. An emotion so new I'd not even known the truth of it until I saw her kneeling by that water, facing her fears so bravely.

Without a word, I drop down by her side, seeing the bow and quiver for the first time. She followed me out here. To hunt. To show me she is capable.

And I am naught but your wife, so you may tell me what to do. Just like my father.

Holding her as she releases the tears that come after a person has done something terrifying, like approach a stream alone for the first time after having seen their sister carried away by the current, I murmur words she likely does not hear.

"I am sorry, Reyne," I say, over and over again.

For her sister's loss. For lying to her those first few days. For treating her differently than Cettina. For thinking not making love to her would do anything more than punish us both.

"I am so very sorry."

We stand together, and I wipe the tears from her cheeks.

"I love you, Reyne." It is so easy to say the words when they are true.

I pull her away so that I may look at her face.

"And am glad you are here, even though I do worry for your safety. And I'm so proud of you. How scared you must have been to kneel down there as you did."

Wetness still glistens in her eyes.

"I grabbed my bow," she says, "and followed you. I did not

realize . . ." She looks down at the stream as I would toward my enemy. "I did not realize it was here."

And then her head snaps back.

"Did you say . . . ?"

It was as if she'd listened to the words but only heard them now.

I nod.

"I love you," I say again so she need not doubt herself.

Her lips part, and though I think, hope, she will say it back, Reyne does something more potent. She stands on her toes and reaches her lips to mine. The touch is soft, hesitant, at first. But when I deepen the kiss, taking her in my arms, all sweetness flees as surely as the deer we hunted.

Too quickly, I am lost in her. My hands cup her buttocks, so easily done in her breeches. It takes no time for me to grow hard, my need for her overwhelming. Even so, I made a vow to my wife, and my hands remain where they are.

Until she presses me toward her, lifting my long surcoat up from the back. I step away to assist her, and am lost when Reyne smiles and nods.

Lowering us both to the grass, I kiss her with everything that I am. Our tongues swirl together, as one, and I mourn that our first time together will not be as I had hoped. Night is coming, and while I'd strip my wife of every item of clothing she wears, keeping her safe this night is more important.

Not willing to wait another moment, I remove my boots quickly as Reyne sits up and does the same. I think to take off at least my hose but the look she gives me does not allow it. Instead, I kneel down beside her and take advantage of her peculiar women's clothing. As my lips cover hers once again, I work open her braies and dip my fingers inside, anxious for her to know a new kind of pleasure.

When she gasps against my mouth at the first touch, I do

not relent. Instead, I tell her with our kiss that such a thing between man and wife is acceptable. My fingers move in rhythm with my tongue, surging and retreating until she grasps the material at my arm so tightly, I know she is about to find release.

When she does, it is glorious. She cries out, and I break our kiss to let her. Eyes wide, her lips parted, Reyne looks down at my hand, which is still inside her breeches.

Not for long.

I remove it and pull the breeches down completely. Reyne kicks them off and continues to stare up at me.

"This is not at all what I envisioned our first time would be like," I say, my voice low. "If you'd prefer, we can wait."

She looks around us, and only when we are both silent do I hear the water nearby and realize the significance of this place.

"It is perfect," she says, smiling like a woman well pleased. As I reach down to free myself, now straining and very much ready to make love to my wife, a sound in the distance startles us both.

Immediately on my feet, my sword out and at the ready, I'm prepared to face the intruder, until I see Reyne creeping toward her discarded bow and realize this is no intruder, but the deer.

A buck.

One who miraculously does not see us. Quietly, I lower my sword and watch as Reyne moves her bow into position. As she nocks her arrow, I ingrain the sight before me, one for a lifetime. Lady Reyne Moray, legs and feet bare, her surcoat falling just low enough to cover her bottom, aims. The waning sun touches her hair, glinting off a piece of metal, and though I cannot see it clearly at this distance, I know it is the pin she favors, the one with the Kona she purchased from the Garra that second day.

Watching her rather than the deer, I only shift my attention to the woods after she releases the arrow. Seeing nothing, I can nevertheless hear the distant thwack of her arrow connecting with the target. We wait, and listen.

"You got him," I say finally as Reyne realizes what she is wearing. The sight of her laughing, barefoot and barelegged, having just shot a buck, not even realizing how close she is to the riverbank, *almost* distracts me from the thought that, instead of consummating our marriage, I will now be dragging a buck back to camp.

ERIK

*W*e finally arrive at Carwell Castle.

The journey is torturous—made so by exchanged glances, innocent touches as we sit together at the fire for meals, and not-so-innocent touches during the few hours my wife and I have had in between late-night watches and early-morning rousings—and I am more than ready to stomp out this rebellion, arrest Rawlins and Whitley both, and make love to my wife.

Although not necessarily in that order.

In fact, as the towers of the castle come into view, my thoughts are firmly fixed on the latter as I wait for Reyne, who rides in the rear alongside the queen. Our riding party will be able to sleep tonight, within the safety of the castle walls.

Or at least the others will rest.

I look forward to *not* resting. Tonight I intend to make good on the promise I made to Reyne this morn as we woke.

"This night, you will be mine in every way."

I had thought she was sleeping, but as I pulled back the

flap of our tent, no light streaming inside just yet, my sleeping wife whispered, "As you will be mine."

Smiling like a fool the rest of the morn, and grateful our journey had been an uneventful one, I saw Reyne just once that day. We pushed hard, knowing Carwell was within our reach. Watching now as the men ride past, I urge my mount forward so that I might find Reyne and Cettina. My wife's face lights up when she sees me, and I feel a reflection of that light within me. I turn and my horse falls in next to Reyne's mount. It is then I greet Cettina, who appears worried.

"When will the scouts return?" the queen asks.

I break my gaze with Reyne to answer.

"Those to the west and east may already be within the castle walls. But I don't expect those across the river just yet."

By arriving early, we've time to scour the area surrounding Craighcebor and Firley Dinch too, before Rawlins and Whitley are due to attack. Doing so without alerting anyone beyond Carwell of our presence will be as tricky as containing the information we are staying at the castle.

The Curia agreed Lord Carwell, a loyalist to the crown, could be trusted, and even now the gates are being secured. No one in, or out, of these walls until this is all over. Any who question the reason will be told a sickness is within, a regular enough occurrence that it will not raise suspicions.

"I would speak with Lord Carwell immediately," she says.

"Of course."

Cettina spurs her mount ahead without a backward glance.

"This is suddenly so real," Reyne says, "not just some discussion of traitors and battles." She swallows. "Will you be safe, Erik?"

"Aye." And then, remembering I vowed never again to lie to her, I amend my answer. "As safe as one can be in a battle.

You are the daughter of a warrior and know the way of things, Reyne."

We ride across the drawbridge, a wet moat under us. One Reyne does not so much as glance at.

"We will know more in the coming days," I add.

I can tell she's worried, but I've no words of comfort for her. The truth is we have only the word of a man who admitted to his involvement in the Saitford slaughter. In truth, I worry more that naught will happen. We will be forced to move against Rawlins and Whitley with little proof of wrongdoing other than a few whispered words and a secret meeting at the tournament.

Enough for an arrest? Aye. But to quell the chest pounding of noblemen unhappy with a woman as their leader? Likely not.

I am about to tell Reyne how we might distract ourselves this eve when Scott appears from seemingly nowhere, having apparently ridden forward from the back as we approached.

"Stokerton," he says in the gruff manner to which I've become accustomed. "We need you in the hall. Immediately."

He says nothing more.

Although we have not yet reached the inner courtyard yet, Carwell is a large circle and easy to navigate, so I respond to the urgency of his tone and say to Reyne, "You will be well taken care of here."

"Go," she says, "I will find Gille."

I don't see my friend but know he is somewhere behind us. Perhaps I should have taken Bradyn. The poor boy begged to come, but someone needs to keep Breywood safe while we are gone. He did not believe my excuse for a moment, but I have Reyne to protect now and cannot worry about both of them. There are too many uncertainties with this mission.

"Go," she repeats.

I follow Scott through the second, smaller, gatehouse and into the inner courtyard. He leads me to the stables, and we both dismount in quick succession. Handing off our reins, I follow him into the keep, which he has obviously already entered. Like most here along the border, it is tall and rectangular, impossible to properly enter without a ladder.

Thankfully, more permanent stone steps have been added since the original keep was fortified by two curtain walls. We climb them now, Scott yelling back down to me.

"The queen is inside already. With a visitor."

I think immediately of her sister. But of course it is not Lady Hilla. She doesn't know we're here. In fact, none but Lord Carwell and his men knew of our attention. We were careful to avoid well-traveled roads, so who is this visitor?

"Who?" I ask as Scott leads me through an arched but open doorway into darkness. Have they no knowledge of torches and candlelight here? Following the only bit of light ahead, we emerge into the great hall.

There, seated on a dais, is Lord Carwell, a border lord whose family has retained this castle since the days when the two kingdoms were one. Despite its location, Carwell Castle has managed to avoid being overtaken due to their control of the bridge. They collect taxes from those who would cross. The Carwells' support of the kings of Edingham extends from those sovereigns' tolerance of this tactic.

I'd not seen the man in years, but he had been old then, and is even older now.

By his side, in a high-backed chair as ornate as his own, sat Cettina. And in front of them both, his back to me . . . nay, it could not be.

"There he is," Cettina says. "Will you speak to us now?" she asks as the hooded Elderman turns toward me. But I don't need to see Father Aiken's face to recognize him.

"I will speak to Stokerton, and he alone," the priest says.

Such flagrant disregard for the queen's authority, and that of our host, to whom I incline my head in greeting, makes me rash.

"That is my queen," I remind him. "Anything you say to me, you say to her as well."

That his hood is still raised is an insult I'm willing to forgive, but his disrespect to Cettina cannot stand.

"Would you dismiss King Malcom so easily?"

He doesn't flinch. "Aye."

"Try again. And don't neglect our host."

"Your host," he emphasizes. "I am here but briefly, to bring you news."

Cettina waves me off, but she is disrespected enough behind her back. I'll not allow it to happen in front of me. Or her.

"I am but her representative," I say.

Father Aiken looks from me back to Cettina, and then to Lord Carwell. Something in him seems to give, and he nods once, a slight but definitive movement. Cettina and Carwell send all others from the hall, including Scott, who is rightfully displeased as he outranks me. But he says nothing as he leaves the room.

Only then does Father Aiken remove his hood.

"How did you know we were here?" I ask the priest.

"They move in two days' time," he says, ignoring my question. "Rawlins has retreated back to Hempswood, apparently thinking better of his involvement despite that Saitford was his doing. Whitley nearly called off the attack, angry over Rawlins's retreat, but instead he means to move forward without the twenty men Rawlins was to provide."

Cettina leans forward. "So Whitley is here already?"

"Aye. He and his men are scattered throughout the village with their supporters."

"How many?"

"No more than fifty."

"Do they suspect us? Is that why Rawlins retreated?" Cettina asks as I move forward to stand between her and Father Aiken.

"They do not. Rawlins retreated because he is a coward."

He says it as a statement of fact, not opinion. And I'm reminded once again how dangerous this man is, and what he's done in the past, in the Prima's name.

He is not a man I'd trust if given the choice.

"Whitley is a fool *and* a coward," Cettina says, her voice nearly as deadly frightening as the Elderman's.

Father Aiken reveals nothing of his opinion of Cettina's brother-in-law.

"Why do you help us?" she asks him. "And why does

Father Silvester wish to start a war between Edingham and Meria?"

The priest lacks expression as he studies her. "Because Lord Hinton has made a formal declaration that he intends to fight King Galfrid for his crown."

No words could have surprised the three of us more. I think of my meeting with the king's commander, Lord d'Abella, in Murwood End.

"Galfrid is reluctant to name Hinton as heir, but the man is gathering support from the church. The same church that crosses the border. Hinton will be no friend to the queen."

"Who will King Galfrid name instead?" I had asked.

"I do not know."

"Father Silvester," I say now, "wishes for war as a means to help Lord Hinton secure the crown. Turn the people against a king who cannot control the borders. Turn the king's attention away from his usurper."

Again, no reaction.

"Hardly a usurper," Father Aiken says tonelessly, "as the king's closest relative."

Though no fan of the king's, Cettina defends him now. "Their laws are the same as ours. The successor is chosen."

But the priest does not seem to care.

"I came to tell you of the attack. And I've done so." He bows to Cettina, surprising me. "I will take my leave."

Pulling up his hood, Father Aiken turns to leave. But I have too many unanswered questions to let him do so. Following him, I fall in step beside him as he makes his way toward the exit. Since the hall has been cleared, not even a single servant remaining, we each pull open one of the two massive doors at its entrance, startling Cettina's guards.

"Why do you warn us?" I ask as we slip back into the darkness, the corridor leading outside as good a place as any for such a private discussion away from the guards.

"My reasons are my own," he says.

So I try again. "You are a Shadow Warrior."

Father Aiken does not deny it.

"Sworn to protect and defend the Prima. A man who attempts to overthrow a king, killing innocents to accomplish such a thing. What has Lord Hinton promised him?"

Nothing.

"How did you find us?" Before he refuses to respond, I add, "I would know if our position is already compromised."

The faintest hint of a frown is his only reaction.

"It is not," he says finally.

Then, just like the day in the woods, he stalks off silently, the quiet left behind him the only reason I can hear his muttered words.

"My loyalty is to the church. Not the Prima."

Then he is gone. And we've a battle, or an ambush, to prepare for. But my instincts, which I've doubted since the Hilla affair and must learn to trust again, tell me it is the former we are walking into, not the latter.

For his own reasons, this priest, this trained assassin, has chosen to help us once again. And though it seems Rawlins may have slipped through our fingers for the time being, Lord Whitley will not. He will pay for his role in Saitford. For his cruelty toward Lady Hilla.

For his treason against my queen.

*M*y eyes close against their will.

Erik told me not to wait for him, that the new information delivered by Father Aiken would require them to plan well into the night. The last of the scouts arrived just after supper, marking an early end to our meal.

As I drift into sleep, I imagine Erik and the others, including Cettina, gathered in the solar down below, and am proud not to feel even a twinge of jealousy. Though she is the same woman I met that first day, *I* have changed. That moment by the river transformed me, and now I feel nothing but gratitude for the queen's friendship and love for my husband.

Perhaps tomorrow . . .

As darkness descends, I dream of the first night we slept in the same tent. I dream he is lying next to me, his hand resting on my hip, his thumb tracing circles there before gliding from my hip toward the hem of my shift. Then up, inside, simultaneously parting my legs and finding that most intimate part of me. But his hand doesn't remain still for long. As they did at the lake, Erik's clever fingers glide inside of me.

With his palm still cupped on me, he begins to move, and I pray this dream doesn't end.

Only . . . is this a dream? His kiss on my neck feels so real. As does what he's doing with his hands.

I open my eyes. Mostly darkness greets me. Darkness, a single lit candle, and . . .

I try to turn around, and as I do, his hand pulls away. I've no time to mourn its loss as Erik lifts my shift upward. By the time it's discarded, he's above me. Completely nude, his glorious body on full display.

I look down and have little time to react, or to become worried about how precisely this will happen without a considerable amount of pain based on what I just saw, because Erik wraps his hand around himself at the same time as he nudges my legs open.

"This isn't a dream." My voice is thick and hardly audible.

"For me it is, aye."

He positions himself as I brace for the pain I know will accompany this first time.

"Are you awake now, Reyne?"

His gruff voice is my undoing. I've waited for so long, I forget to be afraid. I squeeze my buttocks together in anticipation and lift my hips to meet him.

With a pained groan, Erik guides himself into me and stops when he reaches my barrier. I squeeze my eyes shut, anticipating the pain, and Erik thrusts forward. I buck from the bed, but the stinging is not so bad as I expected. When I open my eyes, the concern I see in his gaze has me reaching for him. When I pull my husband closer, he begins to move.

"Does it hurt still?" With one arm propping his body up, Erik waits for me to respond.

"Nay." I push my hips toward him again.

As if releasing his own restraint, Erik moves with more purpose then. The fullness of him inside me, the knowledge that we are indeed, finally, man and wife . . .

"You watch me," I manage just before he descends. His kiss is swift, and all-consuming. I kiss my husband back, our tongues swirling as our bodies move in the same rhythm.

When he circles his hips, I grip his shoulders. But they are too wide for me to hang on to them. His arms, not much better. I must grip something.

The coverlet will do.

He breaks away then and responds to a question I'd forgotten about.

"Aye, I watch you. Your eyes, so full of expression."

Circling and thrusting, he is relentless.

"Your lips—" he reaches up, "—your hair, so like the fire inside you. All of it, Reyne. All of it, all of you, is now mine."

I cannot hold on much longer.

"As I am yours," he continues. "Let yourself go."

And so I do. He captures the sound I'd have made with his mouth as my buttocks clench and my core throbs in pleasure. When he grunts against my mouth, the vibrations of it not unlike those between us, I know he has found pleasure in me as well.

Collapsing atop me and then rolling us over, still joined, Erik buries his head into my neck. I cannot hold him tightly enough. Knowing what I do now, I want to ask how he could have waited so long. And I want to ask when he will leave me. I want to ask so much, but instead, I say nothing, not willing to let this dream end just yet.

ERIK

The battle was won too quickly to even be called a battle. We waited all night in the thicket across the bridge, on Merian soil, and the traitors arrived just before sunrise. Part of me was astonished the Elderman had not betrayed us. Another part of me was not surprised at all.

My instincts, on this at least, did not mislead me.

When they crossed the bridge, Lord Scott and I led two groups of men in opposite directions, waiting for all of the men to cross before we acted. The moment they did, we emerged from the trees and flanked the bastards on both sides. Not a single sword was raised. They had nowhere to run, for a third group of men already blocked the bridge from behind.

Unfortunately, as the men toss their weapons to the ground, I can see neither Rawlins nor Whitley were among them. While we went into this knowing Rawlins had already scurried home, Cettina and I had hoped Whitley might appear.

The highest-ranking man among them, and the only noble, now stands across from me with Scott and Gille as witnesses. Although Scott outranks me, he has deferred to me as the one who uncovered the plot.

"You have one chance here, MacKinnish," I say. "Tell us who else planned the attack with you, and your family will retain their lands."

The Highlander has a wife and four children, a fact I'd made sure to learn after I saw him at the meeting in Ledenhill.

"Either way, you die a traitor." I don't say anything the man doesn't already know.

He remains silent.

My sword is out so quickly, pressing against the base of his chin, he doesn't have an opportunity to stumble out of its way. His hands tied behind his back, MacKinnish stares defiantly down the tip of the sword.

"She is a fool," he says in response. Assuming he means the queen, I press a bit harder until a drop of blood appears. "They attempt an attack with over two hundred men, and she does nothing?" He heaves a bitter laugh. "Her father may have been mad, but he at least knew how to lead men."

From the way he emphasizes the last word, his meaning is clear. He is the sort who would never follow a woman.

McGreghere makes a sound of contempt. "You are no man. A *man* doesn't kill women and children."

MacKinnish looks only at me.

"You will die for your insolence," I say. "Your ignorance shall go to the grave with you. One last chance, MacKinnish."

Blood continues to drip down his chin, but still he doesn't speak. So I bait him with our knowledge of the plot.

"Your ill-fated meeting at Ledenhill gave us everything we need to know."

The glint in his eyes says my barb has hit its mark. I press him by adding, "We know Rawlins is involved, and Whitley too."

He is surprised, but I have another surprise for him as well.

"You call the queen a fool. But did you think the Prima's help wouldn't come at a price? Once a power-hungry man like Hinton is king of Meria, do you truly think he will respect the borders?" I wave to the river behind us. "You kill innocents to start a war without thinking ahead to Silvester's final plans. What do you think *he* wants?"

It is clear MacKinnish never once considered it.

"He wants all of it. The Isle, under *his* control. First he took Avalon from King Galfrid."

"The king gave it to him," MacKinnish counters, defensive.

"An act even King Malcom knew was foolish. Trusting Silvester has been one of Galfrid's biggest mistakes. But he knows that now. He's shunned him these past years, much as Queen Cettina has done, and so the Prima is retaliating by backing Hinton. A cruel, weak man, as well you know. He will easily control him as he thinks to control the queen by recruiting fools like you to do his bidding. To start a war so that he may take advantage."

A look of horror dawns in his eyes, and I know he finally understands what he has done.

"You have been played, MacKinnish. And where are the Shadow Warriors who were to help you slaughter innocent Merians this day? Not dumb enough to have been caught, like you."

Though he says nothing, his eyes reveal the truth. That I guessed correctly and the Prima's men are out there somewhere, with or without Father Aiken.

MacKinnish will reveal nothing else. It seems Lord Whitley has slipped through our net, and Cettina will not be pleased.

"Take him," I say to Gille, turning back toward the others.

It is then MacKinnish stops me. "He is already there, in the village. Look in the blacksmith's shop."

Not at all where I'd have looked for him. I turn. "If your words are true, your family will be spared the indignity of losing their home."

I look to McGreghere. "Fancy a visit to Firley Dinch's forge?"

*T*he bed sags under me, and this time, I am immediately awakened. Spinning toward him, I throw my arms around my husband. My heart thuds so loudly, surely he must hear it.

"I've been so worried," I confess against his shoulder.

Moving the hair at my neck, he kisses my flesh, murmuring something. The vestiges of sleep are still with me, but as we embrace, I am beginning to become more aware. He smells of fresh water. Indeed, his hair is still damp.

Erik is wearing absolutely nothing, a fact I realize as he tightens his arms around me and pulls me closer. When the others arrived just before supper, Erik not among them, I nearly dropped to my knees in despair. Searching every face, I struggled to breathe as Cettina approached me.

"He is unhurt," she said, reaching for my shoulder as if to steady me. "Erik will be back soon."

"Did you find him?" I ask now, pulling back slightly.

"Aye," he says. "'Twas as MacKinnish said. He was hiding, coward that he is, in the back of the blacksmith's shop. He refuses to confess to his part as one of the organizers of the attack.

The queen's brother-in-law currently slumbers in Carwell's dungeons."

"And Lady Hilla?"

He frowns then, and I realize something is wrong.

"She will be discovered soon."

"Discovered? I do not understand."

Erik appears dismayed, with good reason it seems.

"She was spotted with him in Craighcebor but seems to have vanished."

"Vanished?" My chest tightens. "Cettina must be so worried."

"Worried? Nay, she is incensed. A search party has been sent out, and we will likely remain here until she's found. Whitley was known to have kept her close, but the idea she accompanied him into Craighcebor . . ."

My jaw drops. "You don't think . . . I mean to say, people do not think she was complicit in this?"

His eyes reveal that, aye, some think that very thing.

"Those who know her do not. But as you can imagine, the villagers were not very happy to learn of what almost happened there. Nor is the Merian constable, whose authority it falls under, so eager to exonerate her. And there is the matter of Whitley claiming he did it in his wife's name, to place her on the throne. At her request."

I gasp. That cannot be so.

"But surely, since you stopped the attack. And the queen loves her sister. Would she . . ." I know not what else to say. These are Merians we discuss. Edingham's enemies. They already suffered one brutal attack, and a second was only narrowly averted. Will they so easily forgive a woman they thought may have been in league with her husband? Even if that woman is the queen's sister?

"We will find her," he says, smiling. The corners of Erik's eyes crinkle as he looks down at me.

"I am here now. Lady Hilla will be found, and her husband tried for treason. All will be well."

"I was so scared," I admit.

When he kisses me, I can almost forget. But the throbbing in my temples reminds me of the stresses of this past day. I'm surprised I had even fallen asleep.

"Headache?"

I nod.

Releasing me, Erik lowers me back onto the pillow and presses his thumbs to my temples.

"Close your eyes."

I comply.

As he circles his thumbs, I remember the last time my head hurt this much.

Erik chuckles as if he sees the memory floating through my mind.

"I still must show you how to start a fire," he says, his body propped up next to me, partially covering mine. I smile, my eyes still closed.

"I was just thinking of that," I confess.

He stops rubbing, so my eyes fly open.

"There is another remedy I failed to mention that day."

When he leans down, his lips coaxing mine open, I think I know which remedy he refers to.

"I had not heard of lovemaking as a remedy for a headache before, but I'm willing to see if it might work."

"Are you now? And how do you know that's the remedy I refer to, my saucy wife?"

Smiling, I pull my husband back down atop me.

"Was it not?"

His smile contents my heart, and then he kisses me, and

the worry I've felt all day is replaced with love and hope. For us, for Cettina . . .

And for Edingham.

EPILOGUE
ERIK

When I walk into the hall, having been told on my way abovestairs Reyne could be found there despite the late hour, I'm unprepared for the sight before me. Laughing at something the lord of Carwell says, her head tipped back and hands covering her face, my wife is the epitome of a Highland bride.

That the ladies at court consider reservation in temperament a desirable quality has always been off-putting to me. A Highland woman cares little for hiding her emotions, very much like her male counterparts. There are exceptions, of course, but I'm glad Reyne isn't one of them.

I pause at the threshold, leaning against the wall, content to watch her game of chess with the elderly lord. A friend to the crown, as tough a Borderer as they come, he is well respected and clearly enamored with my wife. Again he says something to make her laugh, and I cannot help but smile at the sight.

"My lord?"

A young servant pauses beside me, and I put my finger to my lips.

"I'd not disturb them. It seems my wife is enjoying your lord's company quite well."

The young man nods. "They've been there since supper ended. She beat him once already, lord, and I fear he'll not let her leave until he is avenged."

"Hmmm," I murmur as the boy walks away. It seems if I do not disturb their game, I might be standing here well into the night.

And after the day I've had, there are other things I would much prefer to be doing with my wife. Considering them, I walk forward, and my presence in the otherwise empty hall is finally noticed.

The smile on Reyne's face lifts my mood, something that shouldn't be possible. But apparently it doesn't soften my expression, because Carwell takes one look at me and asks, "Does your husband always look so grim?"

Reyne reaches her hand up to me as I get close. I take it and stand beside her.

"Nay, the very opposite," she says, continuing to hold my hand. "The news is not good?" she guesses.

"It is not."

She and Carwell look up at me expectantly. I squeeze her hand gently.

"She has simply vanished," I say of Lady Hilla. While the queen returned to the capital with our captives, I stayed on, at Cettina's request, to continue the search for her sister. "We found the traveler and his son who claimed to have seen her on a road just outside of Craighcebor. They recognized her only because the father met her once at court. A mercenary, apparently."

There was more, but nothing else that I was willing to mention in front of Lord Carwell.

"But that was before the attack," I added. "No one we spoke to has seen her since."

"And her husband claims to know nothing of her whereabouts," Reyne finished.

Carwell makes a disgusted sound. "A bastard, to be sure, to blame her when we all know his ambitions are outweighed only by Lord Hinton's in Meria."

"Any news of the king's nephew?" I think to ask. Borderers oft learn of events across the river more quickly than we do in the capital.

"Since he made a formal claim for the throne, backed by the church? Nay."

"Troubling times indeed," I say, wanting to be grateful for Meria's instability but knowing that we inhabit the same Isle, and a Meria in turmoil helps Edingham not at all.

"Checkmate."

While we spoke, my wife used her one free hand, as I refused to let go of the other, to make her final move. One that apparently took Carwell very much by surprise.

But it did not take me by surprise, not in the least.

"How did you . . . ?" Carwell looks at Reyne and then up at me, as if he might find an answer there. In response, I laugh and pull my wife up from her seat.

"If you will pardon us, Carwell. Now that my wife is done thoroughly routing you at chess, I would borrow her. For the evening."

He waves us away. "Go. I will stay here to lick my wounds in peace."

Reyne lays a hand on his shoulder, a testament to how quickly she's formed a bond with him. "I will give you another opportunity to best me tomorrow, my lord."

"Good eve, Carwell," I say as he nods us away.

As soon as we are out of earshot, I give Reyne a look. "You broke the poor man."

I've not let go of her hand yet and refuse to do so now, despite the look the only serving maid in the hall gives us.

"He will survive," she says with a sidelong gaze. "I am sorry you did not have a better outcome today."

When we round the corner, the torchlights on the corridor wall our only guide, I pull Reyne to me, kissing her. Slowly, as if to explain, without words, how this eve will progress. She touches her tongue to mine, and it is only when the same maid from the hall clears her throat that we break apart.

"Pardon us," Reyne mumbles, but I say nothing as we move away.

"I would beg no pardon for kissing you, Reyne, nor for holding your hand. Certainly not for loving you." I pause to look at her. "I would shout it to all who care to hear, and say it to you until you are weary of hearing it."

Reyne cups my face in her hands and smiles.

"I will never tire of hearing it, Erik Stokerton, just as I will never tire of loving you."

This beautiful, fierce Highland bride is all mine, and I intend to take advantage of the fact, this eve and every one after it.

NOT READY TO LEAVE ERIK AND Reyne just yet? Get the bonus scene at CeceliaMecca.com/borderbonus to read their first meetings through Erik's point of view.

ABOUT THE AUTHOR

Cecelia Mecca is the author of medieval romance, including the Border Series, and sometimes wishes she could be transported back in time to the days of knights and castles. Although the former English teacher's actual home is in Northeast Pennsylvania where she lives with her husband and two children, her online home can be found at Cecelia-Mecca.com. She would love to hear from you.

Made in the USA
Columbia, SC
23 February 2021